JUSTICE FOR LAINE

BADGE OF HONOR: TEXAS HEROES, BOOK 4

SUSAN STOKER

1

"No. Absolutely not," Laine told Mackenzie emphatically.

"Please?"

Laine Parker sighed in exasperation. Mack was her best friend, but sometimes she thought they shouldn't be friends at all. Mackenzie was curvy and outgoing and somehow seemed to light up a room the second she walked in. Laine was almost the exact opposite. She was tall and slender and would rather spend the night at home in her sweats than go out .. . but it was hard to meet a guy that way. Still, they were thick as thieves, went together like peanut butter and jelly, and were like blood sisters.

"I only said I'd come because *you* were going. I have no desire to go out to some random guy's ranch, watch as he takes his shirt off and poses for your charity calendar," Laine told Mack in an irritated tone of voice.

"I know," Mack whined, obviously stressed out. "But my new boss asked me to go with her today to check out the venue for our annual charity ball. I wouldn't normally agree, because it's not like she can't go and look at a ballroom herself, but I'm trying to make sure I stay in her good graces. After Nancy left, we floundered a bit before Loretta got here. I don't want to do anything to make her reconsider her employment choice. And, Laine, this isn't a random guy. Wes works with Daxton. He's a Texas Ranger. It's not like I'm sending you to a Chippendale club or something. Besides, Jack will be there."

Laine took a big gulp of her iced tea, wishing it was something stronger. Mackenzie had asked her to lunch today, and she'd thought it was so her friend could grill her on her lack of a love life. Ever since Mack had fallen in love with her hunky Texas Ranger, she'd been trying extra hard to find Laine a man as well.

"Jack being there isn't a positive in my book. I don't really know *him* either. I know I've met him a few times, but you were always with us. Look, you know I love you, but why do I need to go at all?"

"Seriously?" Mack asked, raising her eyebrows.

"Yeah, seriously."

"Okay, here's the thing. Jack is a great photographer. He's one of the best. We were lucky to get him to take the pictures for the calendar. But you know the kind of men Daxton and his friends are . . . they're manly-men. Alphas. Cops. They're not comfortable stripping and having their picture taken . . . especially for another man." She held up her hand to hold off Laine's protestation. "I know, I know, Jack isn't gay, but it doesn't matter. It's weird for them. Daxton told me straight out that if I wasn't there, he wouldn't have done it. So I *need* you to go so it's not just Wes and Jack. Please? Wes is the last model I need to finish this calendar. I don't have a backup guy, he's it."

Laine put her head on the table in front of her in defeat. It wasn't as if she didn't have the time. As a realtor, she had the luxury of setting her own schedule. She'd cleared her calendar so she could be there with Mack for the shoot. The Petersons had gladly moved the tour of the house they wanted to see until the next day, and the Whispersons had no issue moving their showing *up*. So she had the time blocked off to spend with her best friend.

Picking up her head, she acquiesced. "Okay, but you owe me, Mackenzie."

"Yay!" Mack clapped her hands softly in glee. "It'll be fun. I know how much you love seeing the old ranches. Wes's ranch has been in his family for at least a hundred years. Daxton said every second he's not working a case, he's out there doing what he loves. He's a true cowboy in every sense of the word. In high school and college, he was on the rodeo team. He did that roping thing."

"What roping thing?"

"You know, where they let a cow go and they ride out behind it on a horse and lasso it with a rope . . . mm hmm . . . that's next on our agenda," Mack exclaimed. "We need to go and check out a rodeo."

"We've *been* to a rodeo. We went to one last year," Laine reminded her friend.

"Oh, but we weren't really trying to understand anything, we were just there for the eye candy and so we had an excuse to wear our new boots. We need to go and check out what all the events are."

Laine shook her head. Mack was a goof. She tended to ramble too much and was clumsy as all get-out, but they'd been best friends since middle school. Laine would move heaven and earth for her if she asked, especially after almost losing her to a psycho serial killer. Knowing Mack had found the love of her life made Laine happy, even if she was a bit sad at the same time that she herself hadn't found someone yet.

For so long it'd been just the two of them. They'd make spur-of-the-moment plans, hang out all night at each other's houses, and they were confidants. But Laine could see the writing on the wall. Now that Mack had Dax, he was the center of her life . . . as it should be. They'd tried to find the right man for themselves all of their lives, and now that Mack had, Laine felt as though she was being left behind. It was a difficult thing to get used to.

"What time do I need to be out at his place?" Laine asked Mack, trying to get her back on track.

"Ten. I'm not sure what Jack has planned for the shoot, but he said he'd like to use a barn in a shot, if it works out when he gets there. He's been very good at being able to put the other guys at ease. He can figure out the best place to pose them for the shots that show off their assets. Seriously, Laine, you should see some of the pictures so far. Daxton, of course, is hot, but you'd never guess that under his lab coat, Calder is totally ripped. And Quint? Hot damn. Seriously, they could all quit tomorrow, start their own strip club and make millions."

"What about Hayden?"

Mackenzie smiled an evil smile. "Oh, she didn't want to do it, but I bribed her."

"With what?"

"I promised I wouldn't ask her to go shopping with me for at least six months."

Laine giggled. "No wonder she agreed. The last time you dragged her out, she was traumatized for life."

"That's not true!" Mack protested. "Just because I thought she'd look good in that corset thing and the zipper broke and the manager of the store had to come in and cut her out of it, doesn't mean she was traumatized."

"Uh. Yeah. It does."

"Whatever." Mack waved off the incident.

Laine had heard all about the shopping trip from Hayden one night at the bar. The men had thought it was hysterical, but Hayden had glared daggers at everyone for the rest of the night. She wouldn't admit it out loud, but Laine would've paid big bucks to be a fly on the wall during that incident.

"Anyway, I swear you'd think Hayden was a model by looking at the pictures Jack took of her. They went to the shooting range and he somehow convinced her to take off her deputy's jacket, and the picture I think we're using of her is a profile shot where she's aiming downrange. She's wearing a white tank top and her red hair against it is absolutely beautiful. She wanted to keep it up in the bun she always wears it in, but Jack convinced her to take it down. It's a bit curly and the wind blew at exactly the right time for the shot. It's as if she had a fan in front of her, wafting her hair back perfectly. Seriously, I was jealous as all get-out of her hair. Even though she's the only woman in the calendar, I'm so glad we convinced her to do it. The rest of the guys are gonna crap their pants when they see her. She's usually so . . . mannish. Even I had no idea she was so beautiful. She hides it well."

Laine suddenly looked at her watch. "Crap, I gotta get going. I have an appointment in twenty minutes."

"You going to look at another ranch?" Mackenzie asked, knowing how much her friend loved showing the properties on the outskirts of San Antonio.

Laine wrinkled her nose. "Nope, this one is a plain ol' suburban three bedroom, two bath."

"Poor thing."

"I know, right?"

Mackenzie stood up with Laine and hugged her. "Thank you so much for doing this for me. I swear I wouldn't ask you to go if I didn't think it was important."

"Have you met this Wes guy?" Laine asked Mack, putting her purse strap over her shoulder.

"No, but Daxton says he's easy to work with and he respects him. I guess they're pretty close work friends."

Laine shrugged. "I guess that's as good of a recommendation as the man'll get."

"Damn straight."

They hugged again. "Be safe. I'll call you tomorrow night and you can tell me all about it," Mack said.

"I will. Love you."

"Love you too. Bye."

As Laine headed out to her car, she wondered just what in the world Mackenzie had gotten her into now.

2

LAINE PARKED NEXT TO A LARGE, black pickup truck and turned off her engine. Gazing at the house with her realtor hat on, she was impressed. It was big, two stories with a huge wraparound porch. She didn't know what it was about porches, but they seemed to make a house cozier and homier. She thought the house was probably at least three thousand square feet, maybe more if it went back farther than she could see from the front.

It was painted a steel-blue color, which stood out among the plains surrounding it. There was a large red barn off to the left and fences as far as she could see. A few horses grazed on the land around both the barn and the house. Overall, it looked idyllic, and Laine could almost imagine little kids running around while their mother sat on the porch swing watching them play.

She shook her head. At thirty-seven, she was too old to have mommy regrets. It wasn't that she *couldn't* have kids, she knew women were able to have them later and later nowadays, but she was at a point in her life where kids weren't high on her priority list anymore. It was interesting, however, that with all the houses she'd shown and sold over the years, none had made her think about what she might be missing in her life more than this one.

A knock on the window next to her head made her screech and duck to the right in fright.

Jack. The photographer was standing next to her car, grinning like a maniac. Laine put a hand to her chest and willed her heart to slow. Criminy, he'd scared her.

She opened the door and stepped out, smacking the large man on the shoulder as she stood next to him. "Not cool, Jack."

"Couldn't resist. You were sitting in your car like a zombie."

"Maybe I was thinking."

"Yeah, well, think on someone else's time. I need to get this done so I can go and take pictures of a Quinceañera."

"Have you seen Wes yet?" Laine asked, pocketing her keys. She'd dressed for comfort today, as she did most days, in a pair of well-worn jeans and her old brown cowboy boots. They were scuffed and not that pretty looking, but they were comfortable. She'd learned after her first trip to a ranch, years ago, that sandals or sneakers weren't the best footwear for the uneven ground of a working farm in Texas.

"Not yet, but one of his employees said he was in the barn and that he was expecting me."

"Let's get this over with, yeah?" Laine asked, already walking toward the large open doors to the spacious building. "Do you have a plan?"

"Not yet. I want to see what the inside of this monstrosity looks like . . . see if there's a decent place to take some shots. The light is good this morning, but if it's too dark inside, I'll need to find a more appropriate place outdoors instead."

"How many other cowboy shots have you done for the calendar?" Laine questioned as she matched the photographer's stride.

"Actually, none, they were all more law-enforcement based. The other guys and Hayden aren't exactly the cowboy types. That's why I'm excited about this one. Mackenzie told me this guy's the real deal. I'm thinking if I can get what I want, it might be a good cover picture. We *do* live in Texas, after all."

Laine didn't respond, withholding judgement. She'd known a lot of men in her life who wanted others to think they were stereotypical Texan cowboys, but she could count on one hand the number who she'd actually classify that way. Wearing boots and a Stetson did not make a man a cowboy.

They stopped inside the sliding doors of the barn and waited for their eyes to adjust to the dimmer light. After a few seconds, when she could see clearly, Laine almost gasped at the sight that met them, but managed to refrain.

There were several stalls on either side of the space; most were empty, except for two. There was an obviously pregnant mare in one and a younger colt in another. The loft over their heads held hay bales stacked and ready for the colder months, and on the entire back wall hung various leather tack for the horses and other ranching tools.

But it was the man, who hadn't sensed their presence yet, who stole her breath. He was shirtless, and his jeans rode low on his hips, highlighting his flat, muscular stomach. He was tall, probably a few inches taller than her five-nine, and he wasn't a young guy either . . . which actually relieved Laine. She would've felt uncomfortable if she'd been attracted to someone in his twenties. There wasn't anything wrong with it, but she'd always preferred older men.

His profile was to them as he shoveled manure out of one of the stalls. The muscles in his back and side rolled and stretched as he scooped the waste out of the hay on the floor and into a wheelbarrow next to him. His biceps flexed as he turned back to the empty stall and continued with his chore.

Laine could've stood there all day doing nothing but watching this amazingly beautiful, rugged man work, but Jack was seemingly not as gobsmacked as she was, because he cleared his throat loudly and asked, "Westin King?"

The man at the other end of the barn lifted his head and nodded in greeting when he saw the two of them standing at the door. He rested the shovel against the wall and headed toward them. He grabbed a rag hanging off the rail of another stall and used it to wipe his hands as he walked.

Laine felt as if she was stuck to the floor. He'd obviously been in the barn working for a while, because even though it wasn't exactly hot yet, his chest was covered with a sheen of sweat. He had dark hair, and some strands were stuck to his forehead, and the hair on his neck was wet as well. With the way his jeans fit, Laine could clearly see the mysterious and sexy-as-hell V-muscles that she'd only seen a couple times in her life. Laine had no idea what they were really called, but whatever they were, this man's were highly defined and pointing toward the Promised Land.

His abs were equally as impressive and she could see a clear six-pack that flexed as he came toward her and Jack. Her eyes roamed down his legs, over his well-worn and dirty jeans to the tips of his brown, well-used boots.

"My eyes are up here," he drawled, clearly amused at her intense perusal of his body.

Laine knew she was blushing, and immediately looked up into his face. His eyes were a dark brown, the color of the mahogany desk she had at home, and he had laugh lines around them. His lips were full and pink and currently pulled up into a smile, as if he knew exactly what she was thinking. Which would be extremely embarrassing, since she'd undressed him and had her way with him in her mind during the few seconds it'd taken for him to get to them.

Thank God Jack was there to run interference

before she asked the sexy cowboy to turn around so she could check out his ass.

"Jack Hendershot. It's great to meet you." He held out his hand and the men greeted each other.

"Wes King. Likewise." Then he turned to Laine. "You don't look like any photographer's assistant I've ever seen. Mackenzie?"

She shook her head. "Oh no, I'm Laine, spelled l-a-i-n-e. No y at the end. Laine Parker. Mackenzie is my best friend. She couldn't make it today. I was only coming to keep her company, but then she bailed on me and begged me to still come so you wouldn't feel weird about being half naked with Jack."

Laine froze and forced herself to stop talking. Oh my God. She sounded exactly like Mack. She'd obviously picked up some of the other woman's habit of vomiting out whatever she was thinking when she was nervous. She put her chin down and a hand on her forehead, refusing to look at the man who'd scrambled her brains. She'd never been so embarrassed in all her life.

Wes chuckled, and Laine couldn't help but notice his laugh was just as sexy as the rest of him. "I have to be honest and say I'm extremely glad you aren't Mack."

"You are?" Laine looked at Wes.

He nodded. "Yup. 'Cos I know Mackenzie is taken. It's good to meet you, Laine Parker."

Laine stared at his outstretched hand for a beat, trying to process what he'd just said. He was glad she wasn't Mack because she was taken? Did that mean he had the same immediate attraction to her that she'd had to him? She held out her hand automatically and inwardly groaned at the feel of his calloused hand against her smooth one. Jesus, even his hands were sexy.

Jack nudged her with his shoulder, almost knocking her over, before saying to Wes, "I think this'll work just fine. Do you have any objections to me setting up in here? I need to get my stuff from the car, but it'll just be a few lights to make sure the photos aren't too dark and a reflector disc. I think if we use one of the stalls, it'll be a great backdrop. Maybe afterward we can go outside and find one more location as well, just in case."

"No problem."

"Thanks, I'll be right back."

Laine's head whipped up and she was going to offer to help, so as not to be left alone with this man who made her feel way too much, but Jack was already out the door and headed to his car. She looked at Wes and stuffed both hands in her back pockets to try to prevent herself from doing something crazy, like running her palms up and down his glistening chest.

"So . . . you're a cowboy." She mentally smacked herself in the forehead. She was *such* a dork.

"Yup, among other things. You want to meet Star?"

Assuming he meant the pregnant mare, Laine nodded, thankful he wasn't going to bring up her inappropriate behavior, and that he was keeping whatever it was between them at a low simmer. She shouldn't have been surprised though, not really. This man was a Texas Ranger . . . not a twenty-two-year-old kid straight out of college. He was far too suave to say or do something either demeaning or juvenile.

Wes stood back with an arm out, obviously telling her to precede him. Not wanting to seem rude, Laine headed for the stall, all the while conscious that Wes was behind her. Was he looking at her ass? No. He wouldn't do that . . . would he? She looked back at him. Yup, he was totally checking out her butt.

The thought made her stumble and she would've fallen face first into the hay and dirt at her feet if Wes hadn't caught her elbow.

"Careful."

"Sorry. Wasn't watching where I was going."

Grateful he refrained from commenting further on her clumsiness, she arrived at the gate to Star's stall. Wes leaned up against the door and gestured for Laine to step up on the bottom rung so she could reach over the rails.

"How much longer does she have?" Laine asked, reaching out a hand to pet the beautiful chestnut-brown horse who eagerly came to the door of her stall to greet them.

"Anywhere from a month to a month and a half."

"That much? She looks huge."

"Yeah, but it's actually normal for a horse her size. Here, give her this." Wes held out a carrot he'd grabbed from a bucket behind him. "She'll be your friend for life. She's addicted to them."

Laine held out her hand and took the vegetable from Wes. She held it out to the mare and laughed as Star's horsey lips brushed against her palm when she took it from her. "She's beautiful."

"Yeah."

Laine looked over at Wes. He wasn't looking at the horse, but at her. She immediately felt as if she was fourteen again and Timmy James had told her he thought she was the prettiest girl in school.

"I'm thinking the last stall will work."

Jack's words broke through the spell weaving itself between Wes and Laine. She laughed nervously and stepped off the rail, brushing her palms against her jeans. "What can I do to help?" she asked Jack, hoping he had something for her to do that wouldn't entail her drooling over the man in front of her.

"Here, take this," Jack told her, handing her a silver reflector panel. "It'll only take me about five minutes to set up over here."

Laine grabbed the large, spherical reflector panel that looked like an oversize sun screen people used in their cars. She wandered over to the last stall, watching Jack as if it was the most interesting thing she'd ever seen.

She was completely tongue-tied and had no idea what to say to Wes. She'd been attracted to men before, but not like this. There was something about him that made her lady parts sit up and take notice.

The only thing that made her feel less guilty about the entire situation was that it seemed as though Wes was feeling some of the same things she was. Every time she glanced at him, he was watching her. She couldn't take her eyes off him, and apparently, it was a mutual thing.

Finally, Jack was ready.

"Okay, chicks dig the hat and rope thing, so I'm thinking that's the route we should go. Do you have a preference for if your face is shown in the picture or not?"

"Is that an option?" Wes asked seriously.

Jack shrugged. "Sure. I mean, I don't think any of the other guys cared if their faces were seen or not. The FBI guy said he wasn't going to be doing any more undercover gigs, and the others thought it might be good for their dating life or the image of their respective departments. But it's up to you."

"What do you think?" Wes asked Laine.

"Me?" The word came out as a squeak.

"Yeah, you. What do you find sexier? A faceless cowboy or one where you can see his eyes along with the rest of his body?"

"Um . . . well, it depends."

"On?"

Laine didn't really want to get into it, but both Wes and Jack were looking at her in expectation.

"On whether or not I was married or dating."

"Go on," Wes encouraged when she didn't elaborate.

"I don't know why it makes a difference, but if you must know . . . if I was with someone, I think I'd prefer to not see a model's face. It would allow me to put my own guy's face onto the model . . . so when I fantasized, I'd see the man I loved instead of a stranger."

"And if you were dating the model? Would you prefer single women who bought the calendar to fantasize about a random body or your boyfriend?"

Holy. Crap. Laine couldn't take her eyes away from the hot-as-all-get-out man in front of her. Was he serious? She wasn't sure. But she couldn't help but be honest with him. "If I was dating someone and they were having their picture taken for a sexy publication that I knew horny women of all ages were going to buy to drool over . . . I'd prefer his face to be hidden so he'd be anonymous. They could enjoy his body, but I'd want his face to be all mine."

Wes didn't respond to her, but turned to Jack and said nonchalantly, as if he wasn't rocking her world, "Faceless."

Jack grinned, but stayed professional. "No problem. Go ahead and pick up the rope that's hanging over there on the wall. We'll start with that looped over your shoulder. Do you have a Stetson in here? We'll definitely need that, especially since we're going the anonymous route."

Laine didn't say another word, but watched

silently as Wes followed Jack's instructions, strode to the nearby wall and picked up the rope. She felt the goosebumps pop up on her arms as she thought about Wes's words. Unfortunately, she could feel her nipples harden in response as well. Her body was standing up and taking notice of the sexy-as-hell cowboy in front of her.

The next forty minutes were excruciating for Laine. She hadn't realized how difficult posing for pictures could be. She figured the model just stood around for a bit and that was it. But Jack was a tough taskmaster. He asked Wes to pose in all sorts of positions, most with his head tilted down, shielded by the wide brim of his cowboy hat.

It was the flexing, and the sight of his perspiring chest that made Laine shift where she stood. He was so amazingly sexy, she had a feeling if she was alone with Wes, she wouldn't have been able to control herself . . . and that wasn't like her at all.

What also wasn't like her was thinking about what the cowboy could do with the rope he posed with. She'd never been into bondage, but thinking about Wes lassoing her and tying her hands to one of the stalls as he bent her over and took her from behind, made her face flush with arousal.

Finally, Jack was satisfied with the pictures he'd

gotten inside the barn. They moved outside, where the photographer decided that if Wes leaned against the fence, with the barn and horses grazing in the pasture in the background, it was perfect for a possible cover shot for the calendar. While he set up his cameras again, Wes ambled over to Laine.

"So . . . you're friends with Mackenzie, who is Dax's girlfriend. What else?"

"What else, what?"

"I want to know more about you. How old you are, what you do for a living, favorite color, if you'll go out with me next weekend."

Laine bit her lip and looked up at the man next to her. He wasn't that much taller than her, probably four or five inches. His eyes were pinned to hers; he wasn't distracted by anything going on around them, which was heady. She was used to men—and women, for that matter—being distracted by their phones, other people, the houses they were looking at . . . all sorts of things, so being the recipient of all of Wes's male attention was a bit disconcerting.

"You're awfully forward," Laine said, crossing her arms over her ribcage, trying to act like she wasn't dying to jump in his arms, hook her legs around his waist, and kiss his luscious lips.

One side of those lips quirked up. "I'm no more

forward than you, Ms. Parker. You were undressing me with your eyes the entire time I was posing back there . . . and I can tell you, if we were alone right now, you'd find out how appreciative I am of your eyes on me."

"Uh . . ." Laine was tongue-tied and had no idea how to respond.

"Just tell me you aren't attached," he demanded.

The hell with it. Laine was attracted to him and it seemed as if Wes was attracted right back. Why was she even trying to play coy? "I'm not attached. Thirty-seven—although you're not supposed to ask a woman how old she is—I'm a realtor, purple, and yes."

Her opinion of Wes rose when he followed the conversation easily. "I'm forty-two, you know what I do for a living, I don't have a favorite color, but I'm thinking I'm becoming partial to purple as well . . ." He nodded pointedly at the lilac blouse she was wearing.

Laine looked down and blushed when she could see her nipples showing through the cotton bra she'd worn under her tank top. Dang it. She'd thought she'd gotten herself under control. She usually didn't have a problem with spontaneous nipple hard-ons when she was out and about, but obviously this man was making her body stand up and take notice of him without even trying.

Wes continued, "I'll pick you up at your place Friday night." It was a statement and not a question.

Laine quirked an eyebrow. "You will?"

"Yup."

"And if I won't tell you where I live?"

"Mackenzie will."

Darn it. He was right. "Okay, but I'm only allowing it because you're a Texas Ranger. I typically don't let men know where I live before a first date."

"Smart."

"You ready?" Jack asked from a few steps away.

Once again, Laine was surprised by the other man. It seemed as though when she was with Wes, everything else faded away . . . which was good and bad.

Laine watched as Jack did his thing with Wes for another twenty minutes. The photographer seemed very pleased with Wes, and the shots he'd gotten, and finished up the shoot quickly. He held out his hand to the Ranger. "Thanks for allowing me to interrupt your morning. If you ever want to make some money out of this photo thing, please contact me. Real cowboys are in high demand in the romance novel cover market. You'd make a ton of money without even trying." He chuckled at the horrified look on Wes's face. "Okay, okay, but I had to throw it out there. I know you probably have a ton of stuff to do. I'll send over the best shots for your approval before the calendar goes to print."

"I'd appreciate that."

Jack shrugged. "I figure if you're volunteering your body for charity, it's only fair to allow you to say yes or no to the shots I pick out. It'll probably be a month or so before you see them. I still have a couple more shoots to do for another project, and of course then I have to edit and put together the calendar."

The photographer turned to Laine. "You'll tell Mack that the shoot went well?"

"Yeah, I'll tell her."

"Great. Thanks for coming out today," Jack added.

"I don't think I was that much of a help," Laine countered honestly.

"Oh, I think you were more of an inspiration than anything else." Jack smirked, referring to the sparks flying between her and Wes.

"Whatever," Laine murmured, blushing.

"See you later, Laine. Drive safe going back into

the city," Jack told her seriously as he turned to head back to his car.

"I will, you too," she called out behind him. Laine took a step toward her own car when she was stopped in her tracks by Wes's hand at her elbow.

"Hang on a second . . . please?"

Laine nodded, not sure why she was nervous to be alone with the charismatic man standing next to her, but she was. She waited for him to say something, but he stood silent until Jack's car was headed down his driveway.

Then, still without a word, Wes put one hand on the side of her neck and the other wrapped around her waist, pulling her close. Laine's hands rested on his chest in surprise as his head dropped down to hers. Her fingers flexed against his warm skin and she had two seconds to let it register that his chest was just as hard as she imagined it would be before he moved.

He didn't ask. He didn't hesitate. Wes took her lips as if it was the hundredth time rather than the first. When she gasped in surprise at the electricity she swore she felt as his lips touched hers, he took advantage and surged his tongue inside her mouth.

Tilting her head at his urging, Laine reciprocated enthusiastically, loving his aggressiveness as his tongue dueled with her own. When he sucked on her lower lip and nipped it gently with his teeth, she whimpered. Lord, the man could kiss.

He pulled away, not bothering to look around to see who might have seen them making out. As though pulled by an invisible force, he leaned down and kissed her once more, but with more tenderness than passion this time. His tongue lazily caressed hers, seemingly not in any rush and without making her feel it was merely a way to butter her up to get into her pants.

Finally, he took a step back, keeping his hand on her waist until she got her balance. "I'm looking forward to next weekend," he said in a husky voice.

"Where are we going?"

"It's a surprise."

"But I won't know what to wear."

"Ah, I should've thought of that. Okay, dress casually comfortable, but I'd love to see some skin." Wes's finger ran along the strap of the tank top over her shoulder.

Laine knew she should smack his hand away, but his touch felt so good, she knew she wouldn't.

"Okay, but you should know I get cold easily. I swear I don't know what it is about Texas that when the temperature goes above eighty, the people in charge of the air conditioning in buildings think they need to crank it down to fifty."

"I won't let you get cold."

Lord, it was as if they were having sex, but standing upright . . . and a foot from each other.

"Okay then. Skin, comfy, and casual. I think I can do that."

"Good. Drive safe, and I'll see you Friday around five-thirty."

Laine could only nod as she backed away from Wes. She kept eye contact with him until she reached her car. Fumbling into her pocket for her keys, she finally looked away as she got into the driver's seat.

Driving down the road away from the ranch, Laine looked in the rear-view mirror and saw Wes standing where she'd left him, his eyes on her car as she drove away.

3

"YOU ARE IN BIG TROUBLE, SISTER," Laine told Mackenzie that night when she called to tell her how the photo shoot went.

"Why? What happened?" Mack asked, alarmed.

"You didn't tell me how crazy hot that man was."

There was silence on the phone, which was telling, as Mackenzie was never at a loss for words. After a long moment, she seemed to come back to herself. "What? Are you kidding? I didn't *know*. I mean, we had that discussion in the bar after Quint's girlfriend, Corrie, was rescued. Everyone said he was good looking, but it's not like Daxton would tell me that one of his coworkers was *sexy* or anything. I take it the cowboy thing worked for him? Did you ask him out? Was it weird? How did he act with Jack?"

Used to her friend's nonstop questions, Laine waited until she wound down to speak. "First of all, yes, the cowboy thing worked *really* well for Wes. When we walked into the barn he was shoveling shit out of one of the stalls, shirtless. And let me tell you, I almost had a spontaneous orgasm right then and there."

Laine heard Mack laughing, but went on.

"Jack was cool. But I got sucked into a conversation about whether or not they should take shots that would show his face and Wes actually asked me," Laine's voice dropped, mimicking Wes's low, sexy voice, "'if you were dating the model, would you want your man's face to be shown or not'?"

"He. Did. *Not!*" Mackenzie exclaimed, almost hyperventilating.

"Oh, he did."

"And what did you say?"

"I said that if I was dating someone, I wouldn't want other women to fantasize over my man's face. That they could drool over his body, but his face was all mine. So Wes turned to Jack and told him 'faceless', and so he posed with his hat over his face."

"Holy shitballs."

Laine could understand Mack's reaction, because it was much the same as she'd had standing in front of Wes when he'd asked. "And he's taking me out next Friday."

"Really?"

"Really."

"Truly?"

"Yes, Mack. Truly." Laine heard her friend sniff. "Are you crying? What's wrong?"

"I'm just . . . I'm so happy. I love Daxton with all my heart, but a part of me was sad that you didn't have a man of your own. I've had friends who I've grown apart from because they got married and went on with their married life. I didn't want that ever to happen with us. And I'm just so happy. Because not only are you with Wes, but he's a Texas Ranger just like Daxton. It's like it was meant to be."

"Mack," Laine warned. "This is one date. Don't marry us off yet."

"I know, I know, but this is so *cool*. Where are you going?"

"I don't know. He wouldn't tell me."

"But how do you know what to wear?" Mackenzie asked.

Laine snorted. "I know, right? That's *exactly* what I said! He told me to dress casually, comfortable . . . and to show some skin."

"You know what this means, right?"

"No, what?"

"We get to go shopping!"

Laine laughed at her friend. Shopping wasn't usually her favorite thing to do, but Mackenzie was right, Laine wanted to look her best, and a new outfit that flattered her always made her feel good about herself and gave her a boost of confidence.

THE NEXT WEEK seemed to go by extremely slowly. Monday came quick enough, and Laine and Mack had spent Sunday afternoon at the mall, but between indecisive homebuyers and house inspections that didn't go the way the sellers wanted them to, it'd been a long week. Laine had only gotten to scope out one rural property as well, which was one of her favorite things to do.

But it was *finally* Friday. Laine had left work around noon so she could go home and get ready and try to get rid of her nerves. She'd taken a long bath to relax and dressed in the new pair of Lucky jeans she'd bought the previous weekend. She'd found the perfect blouse for her date as well . . . at least Mackenzie reassured her it was perfect.

It was a dark purple that looked black in low

light. It was sleeveless, with a high neck in the front. It was made of a silky material that draped her flatteringly. It looked modest from the front, but the back scooped down to the middle of her spine, leaving most of her back bare. It wasn't so crass as to dip down to her butt crack, but a nice, modest—if you could call this shirt modest—mid-back drape. A regular bra wouldn't work with the shirt, but there was no way Laine was going without one. Her nipple hard-on fiasco was still fresh in her mind, so she'd made a detour to the lingerie shop in the mall and bought a bra that had one of those versatile straps to it.

Laine refused to get a push-up bra, not wanting to falsely advertise what she didn't have, but she made sure there was adequate padding in the lacy contraption so if (who was she kidding . . . *when*) her nipples peaked, she wouldn't advertise it to the world . . . or Wes. Been there, done that, got the T-shirt. The straps wound around the sides of her ribcage and her lower back, safely tucked away below the drape on the back of the shirt.

It felt sexy and daring . . . and way more aggressive than Laine would've worn in the past. There was something about Wes that made her feel at ease and safe. His profession had something to do with that, of course, but it was ultimately him. He'd obviously been attracted to her, but other than the stolen kiss, he'd controlled himself and hadn't acted like a hormone-driven asshole.

On her feet, she'd strapped a pair of open-toed sandals with a slight heel. Not high enough that she'd have to worry about tripping over her own feet, but enough to give her an extra inch or so. They had a thick block heel and a delicate strap that wound around her ankle.

She couldn't wait to see what Wes had in store for them tonight. Laine had spoken with Mack earlier, promising to call no matter what time she got home that night, as was their custom. It was five twenty-three when her doorbell rang. Laine was glad Wes was early; she couldn't stand when people were late. Her grandmother had been late for everything when Laine was little. They'd usually tell her something started fifteen minutes earlier than it did, just so they could get there on time.

Looking through the peephole to make sure it was Wes before she opened the door, Laine unlocked the deadbolt, opened the thick oak door and stared at the man standing on her stoop.

Wes looked every inch as delicious today as he had the week before. He was wearing a pair of black jeans and a western style shirt that had what looked like snaps up the front of it. It was a deep purple color . . . not as dark as her own shirt, but purple all the same. It figured they matched. They really were on the same wavelength.

The top two buttons of his shirt were open and Laine could see he was wearing a white tee under the button-up top. He had on a pair of what she would call "dress-up boots," as they looked shiny and pristine.

To top off his outfit, he was holding a black Stetson in one hand, and a single purple rose in the other. She had no idea where in the world he'd found a purple rose, but at the moment, she didn't care.

"Hi, you look amazing," Wes observed as she simply stood there staring at him.

His words shook her out of her holy-hell-is-this-man-hot daze. "Oh, yeah. You do too. You want to come in while I get my purse?"

"No. I'll wait here."

"Really?" Laine asked, somewhat confused. His answer wasn't what she'd expected.

"First, even though you invited me, I don't want to overstep my bounds. Second, if I come in, I'm not going to want to leave. So yeah, I'll wait here."

"Oh . . . okay." Somehow she'd forgotten how blunt the man could be.

He held out the rose to her. "Better take this and put it in some water though. Wouldn't want it to die while we're out and about."

Laine reached out and took hold of the rose, bringing it to her nose to smell before telling him, "Thank you. It's beautiful. I'll be right back." She whirled around, leaving the door open, to head back inside to fill a glass of water for the flower and grab her purse.

After a quick trip to the kitchen to fill up a large glass to put the rose in, she went back into the living room where she'd been pacing before Wes arrived, and over to the coffee table. She grabbed her purse and her sweater, which she'd put on the back of her suede couch so she wouldn't forget it, and headed back to her front porch and Wes.

He took a step back as she exited the house and waited patiently as she locked her front door. Laine put her keys in her purse and hooked it over her elbow as she turned back to him. Wes held out his hand, indicating that she precede him down the two stairs and to her front walk-way. She felt his hand on her bare back a split second before he spoke in an almost too-casual way.

"Mind you, I wasn't disappointed in the least when you opened the door, but I was a bit surprised at your choice of attire. I figured your interpretation of 'showing some skin' was different than mine . . . but I was okay with that." Laine felt his thumb caressing her spine as they walked toward his large black truck. "But it's a good thing I turned down your invitation to come into your house, because, darlin', if I'd have seen the back of this shirt before you asked me in, I would've taken you up on it and we wouldn't have left at all."

Laine smiled and looked over her shoulder at him. The compliment was awesome to hear and if she was being honest with herself, she would've been disappointed if he hadn't said anything about it at all. She'd chosen it to on purpose to try to make an impression. It was nice to have that validated. Wes was walking next to her, and she shivered once again as he shifted closer to her and his hand wrapped around her bare side under her shirt, not quite inappropriate-for-a-first-date territory . . . but close.

"We can still go back inside. We haven't left yet," Laine noted enthusiastically. She was all for the dating thing, but with the way she felt while around Wes, and with his warm palm on her side, she could totally do the sex thing first, then the dating thing.

She felt his hand squeeze her waist in reaction to her words, before he relaxed. "Nope. No can do. We're out, and we're staying that way . . . at least for a couple of hours. I've got plans, woman, and your seduction attempts will have to wait."

"*My* seduction attempts? *You* were the one who told me to show some skin," Laine protested weakly, loving his sense of humor.

"You're right, I did," Wes chuckled as he clicked the locks on his truck. He opened the passenger door without another word, finally easing his hand out from under her shirt to hold it out for her to grab on to as she hiked herself up and into the seat. When she was settled, Wes leaned in, resting one arm against the doorframe.

"I don't know what it is about you, Laine Parker. I gave myself a talk before I got out of the truck. I told myself I would keep my hands to myself and be a complete gentleman. But there's just something about you that makes me want to chuck all that away and take you down to the ground and ravish you. I don't know if it's the look in your eye that tells me you want to do the same thing to me, or if it's just some crazy 'it's been too long since I've held a sexy woman in my arms' thing. Whatever it is . . . rest assured, I like it. I like feeling this way. And just so you know, as much as I might want to, I'm not going to make love with you tonight. I find myself wanting to draw out this anticipation. I have a feeling the wait will be worth it. That *you'll* be worth it."

Laine didn't know what to say, she could only sit there with her mouth open in shock as Wes leaned back and shut the door, sealing her inside his truck. As he walked around to the driver's side, Laine muttered to herself, "Holy mother of God. I've hit the mother lode."

4

WES HELD on to Laine's hand as they left the movie theater. He'd done the typical dinner and movie date for their entertainment that evening. It wasn't that unique, but he wanted to put her at ease before they headed back out to his ranch. She knew he was a Texas Ranger, but that didn't mean she should trust him immediately. Just being in law enforcement didn't mean a man was trustworthy, although it should. Nothing pissed him off more than a crooked cop.

He'd been completely bowled over by her tonight. First, standing on her doorstep and getting a look at her bare back as she'd turned away from him almost made him shoot off in his pants. Wes knew he wasn't a young man. While he'd seen his fair share of pretty women in his forty-two years, something about Laine was different, and she turned him on, big-time.

Her shirt, showing off her entire back, wasn't what he'd expected when she'd turned to lock her door, but it was a nice surprise. He'd grilled Dax earlier that week, wanting to know as much information as he could about Laine before their date. Dax didn't say a lot, it wasn't in his nature to gossip, but he did say enough for Wes to understand that she was a good person, and if he played with her emotions, Dax would kick his ass.

It was the implied threat that did the most to convince Wes that Laine was someone he wanted to get to know better. If Dax didn't seem to care if Wes wanted a one-night stand, it would mean Laine wasn't relationship material. It seemed like Laine was a woman who had a good head on her shoulders and she knew what she wanted . . . and as it turned out, it looked like she wanted him as much as he wanted her.

They'd gone to a local hole-in-the-wall steak place that Wes knew about. He'd assisted the owner with a robbery investigation a few years back, and the man hadn't ever forgotten. Wes made a point to eat there as often as possible, which wasn't a hardship since the food was delicious. Laine had laughed without being self-conscious, and had warmly greeted the owner as if he was a millionaire instead of just a humble local restauranteur.

She was good company, eating a hearty dinner and not counting calories, laughing at his stories, contributing to the conversation easily, not bragging about her career, and not acting over the top regarding his. In short, Laine was interesting, funny, sexy, and Wes couldn't wait to get his hands on her.

He hadn't lied to her earlier when he said they wouldn't make love that night. Oh, Wes wanted inside her more than he wanted a lot of things in life, but he was enjoying the heavy glances and the way she made his heart rate increase with every small touch. Wes wanted to draw it out because he knew when he finally got Laine in his bed, it was going to be mind-blowing.

The movie had been an action flick, her choice. The special effects were overdone, as was the acting, but they both knew they weren't really there for the movie. He sat next to Laine with his arm tucked around her waist, his hand under her shirt, as she cuddled into him. Thank goodness he'd had the foresight to choose one of the newer cineplexes that had the rocking seats with the armrests that could be folded up.

Her perfume distracted him from the movie and after it was over, if someone had asked what the plot was, Wes wasn't sure he would've been able to say anything about it with any conviction.

"Thank you for a wonderful night," Laine said as they headed toward his truck in the parking lot.

"Oh, the night isn't over yet. The best part is still to come."

"The best part? Even better than the fried Oreos at dinner? You'll have to try pretty hard to top that one, Ranger."

"Darlin', you haven't seen anything yet." Wes felt Laine shiver at his endearment, but was too much of a gentleman to say anything about it.

He drove them to his ranch, and to her credit, she didn't protest or otherwise tell him to take her home.

When they stopped, she commented dryly, "I thought we weren't going to have sex."

"We aren't. First of all, I said we weren't going to make love, not have sex. I have a feeling it will never be just sex between us. Secondly, I want to show you something . . . and no, it's not in my bedroom," Wes joked before she could comment.

Her snarkiness was just one more thing he liked about her.

Wes grabbed her hand and relaxed when she didn't hesitate to squeeze his in return. "Lead on, oh fearless cowboy. But remember, I'm not wearing my boots."

"You don't have far to walk, just hold on to me and I'll make sure you don't fall." He led them to the barn, grabbing a canvas jacket that was hanging on a hook just inside the double doors. He helped Laine into it then continued, holding on to her hand, to the backside of the large structure, relieved to see the four-wheeler sitting just where he'd asked his foreman to put it when he was done with it for the day. He threw his leg over and looked back at Laine. "Climb on, darlin'."

"Really? Cool!"

Wes was relieved at her reaction. Once upon a time, he'd wanted to do this same thing with another woman he'd just begun to date, and she'd recoiled in horror at the thought of riding through his ranch on the back of an ATV.

He took a deep breath as Laine didn't even hesitate and got on behind him. She immediately wrapped her arms around him and snuggled into his back. Wes took a moment to enjoy the sensation of being in Laine's arms. He could feel her warmth soak into his skin and suddenly had a vision of them lying in bed snuggled together, just like this.

He sat up a bit straighter and put one hand on her thigh next to his, and with the other, he reached behind him and awkwardly wrapped it around her back. They sat like that for a moment, before Wes reached for the handlebars and started the machine.

Being careful not to go too fast so the ride wasn't as bumpy—and to make it last as long as possible—Wes finally pulled up to their destination and cut the engine. They were in the middle of his largest pasture, and once the light to the four-wheeler was cut, it was pitch dark.

"Wow, I didn't realize how dark it could get out here," Laine said with a nervous laugh.

Wes helped her stand, and kept her hand in his. He reached into the bag between the handlebars, pulled out a flashlight and clicked it on. "Yeah, without the moonlight or the city lights, it's tough to navigate. Here, watch your step, we don't have far to go."

Wes kept the light focused on the ground so they wouldn't step into a hole, any cow patties, or trip over any rocks or sticks. Cognizant of the sandals Laine was wearing, he'd wanted to get as close to their destination as possible with the four-wheeler, while still keeping it a secret until the last minute. After a few minutes, he raised the light and showed Laine where he'd been taking them.

"Oh my."

"Is that an 'oh my, this is neat' or an 'oh my, what in the world was he thinking'?'" Wes teased.

"Definitely the former. This is amazing."

Wes shrugged. *This* was two plastic lawn chairs, the kind where you were mostly reclined when you sat in one, sitting side by side. Each had a throw blanket on the seat in case it got too chilly. There was a bottle of wine and two glasses sitting in a small basket next to them. It wasn't fancy, but it was something Wes thought Laine might like.

He'd never admit it, but when he'd talked to Dax about Laine, he'd quizzed him about what she liked to drink. He'd said that she was similar to Mackenzie. No-frills, down-to-earth, and fairly easy to please. He told him what kind of wine he'd see her drinking when she hung out with him and Mackenzie. The last thing Wes wanted to do was offer up a nice romantic gesture, and have it fall flat because she was a recovering alcoholic or she didn't like wine.

Wes walked Laine to the first chair and helped

her get settled. He draped the blanket over her so she was comfortable. Then he poured them each a glass of the specialty wine from the Brennan Vineyards in Comanche, Texas. He clicked off the flashlight, leaving them sitting in the darkness of the evening. Wes waited for her to take a sip, and wasn't disappointed in her reaction.

"How in the world did you know this was one of my favorite wines?"

Wes took a sip of the fruity alcohol and sat back. "I have my ways."

Laine chuckled and sat back herself. "Whatever. You totally asked Mackenzie, didn't you?"

"Maybe."

"Anyway, I guess it doesn't really matter. Thank you. Seriously, this is the best ending to a great date."

"Look up."

"What?" Laine asked in surprise.

"Look up. You'll never find a more beautiful view of the stars than out here in the middle of nowhere."

Laine was silent for a moment as she took in the light show above her head. "Wow. I had no idea. I can see the Milky Way so easily."

"Um hum."

"And Orion's belt, and the big dipper."

Wes could hear her turning in her seat.

"And there, there's the little dipper. Holy cow. This is amazing."

Wes reached over, found her free hand in the darkness and wrapped his fingers around hers. They sat there in silence for quite a while, drinking wine, listening to the sounds of the crickets and other animals around them, and enjoying the serenity of the night.

"Why aren't you married?" Laine's question was whispered, as if she didn't want to break the beauty of the moment. "I mean, you seem like a decent guy." She chuckled to show him she was teasing him. "I don't get it."

"The same reason you're still single, I imagine," Wes told her honestly. "I never found the right woman at the right time. When I was younger, I focused on my career and I thought I'd have lots of time to find someone and start a family. Once I was accepted into the Rangers, I'd been an officer for quite a while, and I guess I'd become cynical. I hadn't run into many women who I could imagine spending the rest of my life with. They were either eager to sleep with a cop, just to say they did, or they weren't at a point in their lives that *they* wanted to settle down."

Laine murmured in agreement. "That's it exactly. I was all ready to pop out two-point-five kids when I was in my twenties, but all the men I met weren't eager to start a family. They wanted to sow their wild oats or some such thing. Then when Mack and I hit our thirties, it was all about our careers and spending time with each other. That sounds bad, but when she moved here leaving me in Houston, I was so lonely without her. We'd become as close as sisters and I was depressed. I'd go straight home from work and spend as much time as possible talking to her on the phone and over the Internet. I finally decided enough was enough and packed up my things and hightailed it down here. Then there was getting used to the new area and trying to get my feet under me and make a name for myself as a realtor here. Not the easiest thing to do, I'll have you know."

Wes squeezed her hand in commiseration. "How are you guys now that she has Dax?"

"Actually, good," Laine told him with no hesitation. "I thought it'd be weird. I mean, she has someone else full time in her life, but she's never, not once, made me feel like a third wheel. Maybe it's because we're older and understand how important friends are. Whatever it is, I'm very grateful."

"You don't resent him?"

"Dax? For what? Loving Mackenzie? Wanting the best for her? Saving her life? Hell no. I love that man as if he's my brother. As far as I'm concerned, I'm writing him into my will."

Wes chuckled and she continued, "Seriously, I'm too old to be jealous, and he gives me no reason to be. I talk to Mack all the time, almost every night still, we get together for girls' night out all the time and he has no issue with us having sleepovers."

They were quiet for a moment, before Wes broke the silence with what had been on his mind all night, certainly since after dinner. "I like you, Laine Parker. I'm not sure why it took so long for us to cross paths, but I swear when I turned around and saw you standing in the doorway to my barn, I wanted to get to know you better. You're easy to be around, you're beautiful and funny, and I just plain enjoy being in your company."

He fell silent, not sure what he was expecting the wonderful woman next to him to say, but he couldn't have held back the words if his life had depended on it. He was too old to play games.

"I thought it was only me. I mean, we obviously have this crazy chemistry, but I like being around you too . . . and not just because you're hot." Laine's words were soft and filled with awe.

"Nope."

"Thank God. But you know what this means, don't you?"

"What, darlin'?"

"I'm going to have to live the rest of my life with Mack gloating and saying she set us up."

Wes laughed and squeezed Laine's hand. "I can live with that."

"Yeah, me too."

They sat in their chairs, looking up at the stars and talking long into the night. Wes finally knew it was time to take Laine home when she didn't answer one of his questions and he looked over and she was sound asleep. He sat, watching her sleep for twenty minutes or so, barely able to make out the features of her face in the darkness, but thanking his lucky stars they'd somehow managed to find each other in the million or so people who lived in San Antonio.

Maybe it was luck. Maybe it was fate. Whatever it was, Wes was going to do what he could to see if they could make it work, because Laine was everything he'd looked for all his life.

5

LAINE LAY in bed and shot off a quick text to Mack. It was late . . . or early, depending on how you looked at it, but she didn't want her friend to worry about her.

Just got home. A.M.A.Z.I.N.G. We'll talk later. Love you.

Laine yawned and put the phone on her nightstand. Mack was either asleep or busy gettin' it on with Dax, and probably wouldn't respond until the morning. She closed her eyes, exhausted, but running high on adrenaline and hormones at the same time.

The kiss Wes had given her at her door had made her wetter than some foreplay she'd had in the past. She'd left the light on before leaving earlier, but after she'd opened her door, Wes had reached around and turned it off, plunging them back into darkness, with only the light from her kitchen faintly illuminating the area around them.

He'd taken her into his arms and proceeded to make love to her mouth—that was the only way to describe how he'd kissed her. Wes's hands had roamed into dangerous territory, quickly learning the intricacies of how she was able to wear a bra with that shirt, but her own hands had wandered too, discovering that he was a briefs man instead of boxers.

Wes had been the one to pull away, regretfully. He'd rested his forehead on hers and moved his hands down to her waist, tucking them under the waistband of her jeans. "Lord, darlin'. You are some-thin' else."

"I take it that's good?"

"Oh yeah, that's good. When can I see you again?" he'd asked, impatience clear in his voice.

"Depends."

"On?"

"On your thoughts on having sex on a second date as opposed to the first."

Laine laughed out loud, the sound echoing off the empty walls, remembering his response. His hands had tightened at her sides and he'd told her, "Dammit, woman. You're killin' me. Tomorrow we have one of those crazy softball games with the firefighters. I'm not on Dax's team, but the Rangers from Division 10 are as much a bunch of cheaters as Dax's firefighter friends from Station 7. After the game, I have to head down to Galveston to interview a witness. I'm not going to get back until late. Sunday night, I'm also working."

Laine had told him that she was extremely busy the next week with house showings and inspections. It seemed like every newlywed in the city wanted her to show them a house in the next seven days.

"Next Saturday," Wes had told her decisively. "Make it happen. You want me to pick you up, or will you meet me at my ranch?"

"I'll meet you there. What time?" Laine didn't even pretend to not want to see him again as much as it seemed he wanted to see *her* again.

"Whenever the fuck you want."

Laine had laughed. "Okay, Wes. I'm looking forward to it."

"It?"

She'd blushed and told him, "Yeah, spending the day with you. What did you think I meant?"

As usual, he didn't hold back his thoughts or his

words. "Spending the day with me. Feeling me deep inside you as you come for me. My tongue on your pussy. My hands all over you."

"Wes!"

"Laine!"

"Lord have mercy."

He'd gotten serious. "You've unleashed a monster, darlin', I hope you know that. I can't wait to see you either. All of you. But yes, I enjoy talking to you and doing nothing with you as well. I do have to get some chores done around the ranch, but maybe you'd be interested in watching and helping with some of them?'

"Of course I would. I'm not just going to sit around while you do all the work."

"I never thought you would."

Wes had kissed her again, hard and brief before letting go and stepping back. "Be safe next week. I'll see you on Saturday."

Laine stretched in her bed and refused to touch herself. She could feel the anticipation building inside, but wanted to wait. The books and movies always said orgasms could be better when they were a long time in coming. She laughed out loud at that. Jeez, what a bad pun. But whatever, she'd hold off and see if the sex with one Wes King was as good in person as it was in her head. Lord help them both if it was.

THE NEXT DAY, Laine sat on Mack's couch, holding a pillow to her chest and trying to explain to Mack exactly how she was feeling about how fast things were moving with her and Wes.

"So there we were, sitting in the dark, looking up at the sky, and all I could think was that I could see myself sitting there forty years in the future, holding his hand and mulling over how great our life had been."

"And? What's wrong with that?" Mackenzie asked seriously.

"What's wrong with it? Mack, I met the man a week ago. That's what's wrong with that. How can I feel deep down that this man is meant to be mine when I just met him?"

"Do you love him?"

"No."

Mack didn't say anything and the silence stretched on, until Laine felt she had to clarify. "I mean, I don't really know him well enough to know if I love him or not."

"You're not fifteen. Or even twenty-two, Laine."

"I know."

"You've dated. You've been in love before."

"Yeah."

"So if you're imagining yourself being with him when you're old and gray, I think you owe it to yourself, and to Wes, to take it seriously. No one's asking you to run off and marry him tomorrow. But don't sell yourself short. Date him. Sleep with him. See how things go. But whatever you do, don't end things before they get started because you're scared you might actually be compatible and could live happily ever after."

"Why do you have to be so damn smart?"

"Because," Mack said smugly. "And you know what else?"

"What?"

"Just remember who set you up."

Laine rolled her eyes and threw the pillow she'd been clutching at Mackenzie. "I knew you were going to go there sooner or later. You didn't actually set us up. You backed out of your commitment and made me go by myself. If he would've been a serial killer, you'd be thinking differently right about now."

"Yeah, well, he wasn't and he's not. And you're gonna get some fantastic sex next weekend . . . so you should be buying me a present every year on that date for forcing you to go without me."

Laine laughed. "You know what? You're right. And I swear, if this ends up good, I'll send you a dozen roses every year on the anniversary of that damn calendar photo shoot in thanks."

"Deal."

The two friends smiled at each other for a beat before Mack leaned over and took Laine in her arms. "I love you. I always wished I had a blood sister, but even if I did, she wouldn't be as wonderful as you are."

"Ditto."

They hugged for a moment before Mackenzie pulled away. "Come on, I'm starved. I think we've got some leftovers we can dig into."

"Sounds good."

"Laine?"

"Yeah."

"You had better call me as soon as you come up for air next weekend."

"I will. You know I will."

6

"You're coming over tomorrow still, right?" Wes asked Laine the following Friday toward the end of their nightly phone call. Even though they'd both been extremely busy, they'd found the time to connect via the phone each night. One night they'd only been able to talk for ten minutes, but another they'd carved out a couple of hours.

"Of course. I thought I'd get there around eleven or so. Is that too early?"

"No. That'll give me enough time to get most of the chores knocked out. I'll talk to my foreman and make sure he's got everything under control, although I have no doubt he will. Want to take a ride with me?"

"A ride? On a horse?"

"Yes. On a horse." Wes laughed.

"Sure, but I should warn you, I'm not that good. I've been on a few trail rides and stuff, but I think the last nag I was on was about four hundred years old. The only thing it was interested in was getting back to the barn and eating some hay."

"I'll take care of you, Laine. I won't let you get hurt."

"Promise?"

"Promise."

"Okay then. But not a long one . . . okay? I don't want to be too sore."

"You got it. I wouldn't do that to you . . . or us. Just a short ride. I need to check the fence line to see if there're any holes or if it otherwise needs repairing, so we'll go nice and easy and take as many breaks as you need. How about we have a picnic lunch while we're out too?"

"You're too good to be true."

"Nah, I just know how hungry I get while I'm riding the fence."

Laine laughed. "Okay, if you say so."

"I'm looking forward to spending time with you. And I'm not just talking about in bed."

"Me too. It's been a long week."

"Very long. It's weird, the things that reminded me of you as I went through my days."

"Really? Like what?"

"Lots of things. A billboard for a winery. A news article about a meteorite shower coming up next week. I pulled over a woman and she was wearing a purple shirt . . . I even let her off with a warning because what she was wearing reminded me so much of you. Hearing one of my fellow Rangers talk about a rodeo."

"A rodeo made you think about me?"

"Yeah . . . rodeo . . . cowboys . . . rope . . . made me think about you eyeballin' me during my photo shoot."

"Whatever, smarty."

"I just wanted you to know that as much as I'm looking forward to seeing you naked on my sheets, I'm just as much looking forward to holding your hand, watching you enjoy your lunch, seeing you interact with Star . . . it's everything. I feel like a little kid who gets to spend all day at the amusement park. I feel like a teenager again, looking forward to a first date. The anticipation is killing me."

"I hope the reality is as good as your expectations," Laine said a bit nervously.

"I have absolutely no doubt it will be. So . . . eleven, right?"

"Yeah. That'll give me time to sleep in, have my three cups of coffee so I can wake up, and to pretty myself up for you."

"Bring an overnight bag."

"I'd planned on it," Laine told Wes without missing a beat.

"Shit. You're perfect."

"Not really, but I'll happily let you think it."

"Have a good rest of the night. I'll see you in the morning," Wes told her in a soft voice.

"You too. Later."

Laine clicked off the phone and smiled. She'd thought a lot about what Mack had told her the other day. It had been very insightful and deep, and she'd been exactly right. Laine decided that whatever happened tomorrow, she wasn't going to sweat it. She liked Wes a lot. He was handsome, sexy, and honorable, and she'd be an idiot to blow him off because she was afraid she liked him too much.

Eleven o'clock couldn't come fast enough.

It was after dinner on Saturday night and Laine lay

in the circle of Wes's arms on his couch. She should've been tired after the long day, but she was wired and more than ready to take her relationship with Wes to the next level.

She'd arrived right at eleven that morning and was met by Wes in front of his house with a toe-curling kiss. He was wearing a tight T-shirt and a pair of jeans with his brown work boots. His ever-present cowboy hat on his head, shading his face from the sun. He'd taken her hand without a word and led her into the barn, where they had a bit more privacy, and proceeded to kiss her to within an inch of her life.

Reluctantly he'd pulled away, and had helped her mount a gentle mare. They'd ridden lazily along the fence line of his large property. Every now and then, he'd stop to make some adjustments to and reinforce parts of the fence. Each time, he'd helped Laine dismount and she'd assisted him where she could.

They'd stopped and had lunch under a few trees on the far north side of the pasture. They'd made out after they'd eaten and Wes had pulled back before they'd gone too far. He'd looked sheepishly at her and said, "I swear I had only planned for us to eat lunch."

He'd been so earnest, all Laine could do was laugh.

They'd arrived back to the barn and made their way into the house. They'd talked some more, eaten a light dinner, and watched a movie. The show had long since been over, but neither had the desire to get up and put in a new one, so they sat in each other's arms, enjoying being together.

"Tell me you feel it too," Wes said during a lull in the conversation.

"What? The anticipation? The electricity? Yeah, I feel it too," Laine reassured him.

"I keep telling myself that it's too soon. I haven't been this interested in a woman in a long time."

"I know. I feel like I should consider myself a slut for even contemplating going to bed with you tonight, but I don't. Not in the least. It feels right." Laine looked up at Wes and put her hand on his face. "Take me to bed?"

"With pleasure," Wes told her, standing up, grabbing hold of her hand as he did.

Laine stood up with him and followed him into his bedroom.

~

WES FELT the adrenaline coursing through his veins. He was more hyped up to see Laine naked for the first time, to feel her skin next to his own, than he was when he tracked down a fugitive. He hadn't really thought about finding a woman he could spend the rest of his life with . . . figuring no one would really want to hole themselves up on his ranch and all that came with being married to a rancher. He wasn't ready to pull out a ring and ask Laine to marry him. But he liked her. A lot. He wanted to spend more time with her . . . not to mention, he really, *really* wanted to get her into his bed.

Reaching behind his neck, Wes pulled his T-shirt off with one quick tug. He smiled as Laine's eyes widened at the sight of his wide chest. Not feeling self-conscious in the least, Wes undid his jeans and pushed them down his legs until he was standing in his boxer-briefs, which left nothing to the imagination. He was way too excited at this point to hide his erection or even try to control it.

Laine reached for the hem of her own shirt and slowly drew it up and over her head. She bit her lip and paused in her disrobing.

Seeing her discomfort, Wes took over, not wanting to do anything to make her feel ill at ease.

He soothed his hands from her shoulders to her wrists and back up. "You're beautiful, Laine. Never doubt that I find you attractive." He ran his palms over her breasts, still covered in her lacy bra. "I'll never forget the sight of you standing in front of me outside my barn, blushing when you realized how hard your nipples were as you'd been gawking at me."

She smiled up at him at that. "I was so embarrassed to know I was showing you a full nipple hard-on."

Wes chuckled. "Nipple hard-on?"

Laine nodded. "Yeah, me and Mack came up with that term in the tenth grade. We'd been at a football game and it was raining. We'd forgotten our jackets and were freezing. A freshman cymbal player looked at us and his eyes got huge. We didn't know what his problem was until we scrutinized each other. We decided our hard nipples were the equivalent to a guy getting a hard-on at an inconvenient time."

Wes smiled at Laine's story while he reached around her back, unhooked her bra, easing it down her arms and dropped it on the floor. He lifted her tits in his hands and gently squeezed, not taking his eyes away from her hard little nipples, amazed when they tightened further in front of his eyes.

"This moment will forever be engrained into my head." He glanced up and looked Laine in the eyes for a moment, before gazing down at his prize again. "My mouth is watering, I want to taste you so badly." He took a step closer to her so she could feel his erection against her lower stomach. "I feel like I could burst just from looking at you, from smelling your arousal." When she moaned, he added, "From listening to the sounds you make."

Wes ran his thumbs over her nipples once . . . then twice, before lowering his hands to her pants. "If I don't get your pants off, I might just do that." He deftly undid the button on her jeans and unzipped them, pushing them, along with her panties, down her legs without missing a beat. "Step out, darlin', then scoot back on the bed."

Wes took care of his own underwear as Laine moved onto his mattress. He noticed her eyes were taking in his body as much as he was taking in hers. She was all woman. Yes, she was tall and slender, but she had an hourglass shape, which made his hands itch to trace her slight curves, and she had a pair of tits that made him want to bury his head between them.

Laine licked her lips and she took her time taking him in as well. "My God, you are gorgeous, Wes. Seriously. I feel like the band geek who somehow managed to snare the quarterback."

Wes crawled over to Laine on his hands and knees and his legs almost gave out when she took his cock in her hand and caressed him.

"You wouldn't have liked me back in high school. I was a self-centered prick who probably wouldn't have taken a second glance at anyone outside my own circle. I know better now. When I see the sexiest realtor I've ever seen in my life, I'm not dumb enough to hesitate to make her mine."

Wes ran his hand from Laine's hip up to her chest, taking her breast in his hand again, pushing it up as he came down onto his elbow next to her. He licked the rosy nipple begging for his touch, watching as her pectoral muscle jumped under his ministrations, before stating, "And make no mistake, Laine, after tonight, you're mine. I'll never get enough of this body . . . of you."

Done talking, Wes leaned down to stake his claim once and for all. He engulfed her nipple in his mouth and sucked, hard, loving how her back arched into his touch. One of her hands came up to grab his naked ass, and the other landed on the back of his head and pushed him harder into her.

He took his time worshiping her breasts. First one nipple, then the other. He licked around the turgid bud then kissed along her collarbone. He nipped her earlobe and blew into her ear, loving how she shivered under him and goosebumps rose on her arms.

She tried several times to reciprocate, but Wes hadn't had nearly enough of her to let her take her turn yet. She apparently got impatient with him taking, but not letting her give anything in return, because she pushed against him hard, and Wes rolled over onto his back.

Laine immediately straddled his stomach and put her hands on his chest. "My turn," she demanded, waiting for him to argue.

The view Laine was giving him was heavenly and Wes had no desire to deny her. He put both hands on her hipbones, letting his thumbs rest in the creases where her legs met her groin . . . close to her folds, but not touching.

Without taking his eyes away from where she was weeping for him, Wes encouraged, "Knock yourself out. But I'm warning you, darlin', you've only got a couple of minutes before I take over again. I need you too much."

She didn't argue, or hesitate. Laine ran her hands down his chest to the hair above his cock, then brought them back up and pinched his nipples. She leaned down, blocking his view of her gorgeous pussy, and sucked one of his small buds into her mouth. The position might have obstructed his view of her, but it also pushed her hips farther down his body. She shifted until she was straddling one of his legs.

Wes swore his vision went black for a moment when she sucked hard on his nipple, snaked one hand down his body until she grasped his hard length, and ground herself against his leg, smearing her wetness on his thigh in the process.

Before he even thought about what he was doing, Wes had pushed Laine over until she was on her back again and he was hovering over her. "God-damn, darlin', you make me lose my head. You're so fucking perfect I can't . . . shit, I can't even talk," he groused as he felt his balls pull up against his body.

"Bad timing, I know, we should've already talked about this," Laine ground out, "but I'm on the pill. I haven't had sex in a year and a half and I'm clean."

"Fuck. I have condoms in the drawer. I meant for

this to go slower. It's been fourteen months for me. I'm clean too. Swear." Wes groaned as Laine arched into him and his cock brushed against the trimmed hair above where he wanted to bury himself. He cleared his throat and rushed his words, wanting to get this part over with so he could experience bliss. "The papers are in a drawer in my kitchen. I'd planned to discuss this with you like a civilized person while we relaxed after dinner."

"Fuck me, Wes. God, please. I've resisted the urge to get off this week because I wanted to wait and see if it made this better. I'm so damn horny I feel like my skin is on fire, and I need to come so bad. Please."

Before the last word was out of her mouth, Wes took hold of the base of his dick and guided his way inside her hot folds. He slipped in easily, her excitement coating his way. They both groaned at the feel of him coming inside. He caught himself on his hands on the mattress next to her shoulders. He closed his eyes, not moving, wanting to memorize the moment.

"Wes?"

"Shhhhhh."

"What are you doing?" Laine whispered.

"I'm imprinting this exact moment to memory."

Wes opened his eyes and looked deep into Laine's. "The first time I am inside you. How perfect it feels. How amazingly, wonderfully perfect this is."

"Wes . . ." Laine's voice trailed off as he pulled almost all the way out and pushed his way back inside.

"As much as I want this to last forever, I'm afraid it's not going to," Wes warned as he continued to thrust in and out of her.

"It's okay, we can do it again."

"There'll never be another first time," Wes told her a bit sadly.

Laine brought her hands up to his face and held it lovingly. "But there'll be a second. And a third. And a fourth. And if we're lucky, a four thousand one hundred and sixty-eighth. Make me come, Wes. I need you."

Her words were all it took for him to let go of the iron control he'd been holding onto. He moved one hand down to where they were joined and used his thumb to press against her clit as he thrust harder into her. "I didn't get the chance to taste you, but I will. That's on my list . . . and you should know, my list of things I want to do with you is getting longer and longer. But for now I want to feel you come apart under me." His thumb was relentless, dipping down to where they were joined to gather her juices, and caressing, rubbing, and pressing down on her sensitive bundle of nerves.

Wes felt her clit swell until the tip peeked out from the hood that usually protected it as she writhed under him. Loving that he could turn her on that much, he sped up his efforts until Laine was shaking on the verge of her orgasm.

He thrust inside her and held himself still as he felt Laine's orgasm explode from the inside out. She gripped his cock so tightly, it was all Wes could do to hold off his own orgasm so he could fully appreciate her ecstasy.

Finally, Laine was only twitching in his grasp instead of out-and-out jerking. He pulled out then slammed back into her. Once. Twice. Then, knowing he was close, bit out, "I'm coming, darlin'. I'm coming." He thrust into her to the hilt and held her to him as his balls drew up close to his skin and he burst forth harder than he'd ever done before.

He vaguely felt Laine's hands running up and down his chest as she caressed him through his orgasm. Wes dropped down lightly onto her, pushing her legs open farther, forcing her to wrap them around him. He felt himself growing soft and mourned the end of their first lovemaking session.

"Don't be sad," Laine said, somehow reading his mind.

"I'm not sad, exactly."

"Then what, exactly?" Laine asked with a smile in her voice.

"Uh . . ." Wes couldn't think. "I guess I *am* sad. I wanted it to last longer."

Laine giggled, and they both groaned when her laughter pushed his flaccid length out of her body. Wes immediately rolled so Laine was resting on top of him.

"What are you doing?"

"Well, since we didn't use a condom, the gallons of jizz that you forced out of my body will, sooner or later, be making its way out of yours. I didn't think you wanted to sleep in the wet spot . . . so I'm trying to be a gentleman here."

"Oh, you goof. Let me up. I'll go take care of things and come back, then neither of us needs to sleep in the gross wet spot."

"I like you here," Wes whined.

Laine pushed up to her hands and knees then leaned down and kissed him, pulling away when he tried to deepen it. "I'll be right back, don't move."

Wes watched in the dim light of the room as Laine hopped off the bed and headed for the bathroom. He thought for the hundredth time that night how lucky he was and how pretty Laine was.

She was back within moments and snuggled into his side. Wes drew the sheet up and over them both and closed his eyes in appreciation for his life.

7

LAINE SMILED down at the text on her phone the next morning while she sat at the table waiting for Wes to finish making their breakfast. He'd insisted on making them both omelets, and Laine didn't argue. Why would she? She'd let Wes cook her every meal if he wanted to.

"What are you smiling about over there?" Wes asked as he carried two plates to the table, putting one down in front of her.

Laine turned her phone so Wes could see the text that Mack sent.

On a scale from 1-10?

Wes's brows furrowed in confusion. "What's that mean?"

Laine looked down at her phone as she typed out

a reply. "She wants to know on a scale of one to ten how the sex was. I told her a seven point five."

Laine screeched as her phone was grabbed out of her hands. "Hey!"

Wes was looking at the screen. "You did not. A twenty?" He grabbed Laine around the torso and tilted her chair until it was resting on the back two legs.

Laine squealed again, holding on to Wes for all she was worth and laughing at the same time. "Wes! Let me up! Of course it was a twenty! Good Lord, man. You were there. Do you disagree?"

Wes kissed her until she couldn't breathe and finally brought her upright. "I would've told her at least a thirty."

Laine snatched her phone back up and read Mack's response.

You're welcome.

They both laughed. Laine relaxed as they ate their breakfast. She'd been a bit worried that the morning after they'd had such awesome sex would be awkward, but it hadn't been. Laine had opened her eyes that morning to find Wes up on an elbow, watching her. He'd smoothed a length of her hair behind her ear and smiled down at her.

"Good morning, sleep well?"

"Yeah. You?"

"Best I've slept in a long time. You make a good pillow."

They'd both laughed and Wes had told her to use the master bathroom and he'd use the guest one. Yes, they'd had sex, but it was still a bit weird to do normal morning stuff with him the morning after, and he'd somehow known it. So they'd taken showers in separate bathrooms and met in the kitchen.

"What are your plans for the day?" Wes asked her after they'd finished eating.

"I have a showing this afternoon. You?"

"I'm assisting in an interrogation of a suspect in a robbery, and I'm on call."

Laine wrinkled her nose.

Wes smiled at her and stood up. He kissed the top of her head and grabbed their dishes. "Such is life for two working adults. But know this, darlin', I'm going to make every effort to see you every time I can. When I've got time off, I want to spend it with you. When you've got the time, I'd love to meet you for lunch. As much as possible, I want to spend the night with you. I don't care if we're both dead on our feet and all we do is sleep, I like being around you."

Laine stood up, followed Wes into the kitchen,

and watched as he nonchalantly rinsed off the dishes and put them into the dishwasher without having to be prompted. It hit her then. Wes wasn't a boy. He was a responsible man, who'd lived on his own for a long time. He wouldn't expect her to cook all the time, or always do their laundry, or clean the dishes . . . he was used to doing those things for himself, just as she was. The perks of dating a man like him occurred to her again. She smiled and came up behind him, wrapping her arms around him and resting her head on his back.

"I'd like that."

"Like what?"

"All of what you just said. Meeting you for lunch. Sleeping with you. Hanging out with you. Spending time with you when we're both free . . . and when I'm not busy hanging out with Mack."

Wes turned in her arms. "I'd never make you choose between me and Mackenzie, Laine. I know how important she is to you."

"Thanks. I know I told you about our close relationship before, but wanted to make sure you really understood.

"Never be afraid to tell me how you feel. As we've said, we're not sixteen. Communication is the key to having a strong relationship."

"Agreed. So we're officially dating?"

"Absolutely." Wes beamed at her, showing off his perfect smile. "So . . . what time is this showing you have this afternoon?"

Laine grinned back at him mischievously. "What time do you have to go into work?"

"Not for a few hours."

"Same here."

Wes started backing her out of the kitchen toward his room. "Looks like we have a few hours on our hands then. Whatever shall we do to pass the time?"

"I might have some ideas," Laine said, then turned and sprinted down the hallway, laughing as she heard Wes pounding after her.

8

I CAN'T WAIT to see you tonight

Laine's lips turned upwards in a small smile at the text. Wes never failed to make her feel good. They'd been dating for a little over a month and everything about him made her happy. He was protective, but not stifling. He was responsible and polite, and he made her laugh. Oh, he'd pissed her off too, but because she immediately called him out on his actions, they worked their way through them when they did occur. Just as he did with her when she said or did something that he wasn't sure about or didn't like.

Me either. I'm going to check out a property then I'm headed to your place.

Be careful. See you soon.

I will. Later.

Laine turned off her cell to save the battery, which was only at twelve percent. She'd forgotten to bring her charger today and she wanted to make sure she had enough juice for her trip back to his place, just in case. Safety first. Wes had gotten upset with her the other week because he'd tried to call her and couldn't get through because her phone was dead. She'd tried to tell him how she was simply too busy to remember to keep her charger with her all the time, and he hadn't listened to her, rightly so. It wasn't a big deal to carry the stupid thing and she was trying to be better at keeping her phone charged. She didn't want to worry Wes and she'd be upset if the shoe was on the other foot and she couldn't get in touch with him if she needed him.

She put her cell back in her purse and climbed out of her car. The ranch took some doing to find, as it was way off the beaten path . . . but it was so worth it. The neglect was obvious, but the property was gorgeous. Laine could see through the neglect to the gem it could be once again. A porch swing was hanging by one chain on the wide screened-in porch on the front of the house. She could hear the banging of a door from somewhere; she assumed it was coming from the large barn off to her right.

The house was one story, a true ranch-style property. There was a large window in the front, which faced west. Laine could almost imagine the beautiful sunsets the previous occupants of the house had enjoyed over the years. The current owner was a ninety-two-year-old woman who'd long since been moved to the city and into a nursing home. She had one daughter who had no desire to live on the ranch. It was kinda sad, as the home had been in the Johnson family's possession since the 1800s. But since there weren't any relatives who wanted it, they had put it up for sale.

There had been several additions over the years and it now boasted five bedrooms and four full baths. The paperwork said it was forty-five hundred square feet, but Laine knew that when the guesthouse square footage was added in, it would easily top six thousand in living space.

It had been on the market for a couple of years, and the daughter was desperate to sell it. The woman had contacted her, wanting to switch to a different realty company, to see if that would breathe new life into the listing and hopefully to sell it.

Laine leaned into her car and grabbed her ever-present boots, remembering how she'd worn them the first time she'd been out to Wes's ranch. The memory made her smile as she tugged off her sandals and put on the socks and boots. She wanted to walk around the entire grounds to get a feel for it personally. She'd found the best way to represent a property someone wanted to sell was to find out all about it . . . pros and cons. If she was upfront with a potential buyer, or another realtor, it went a long way toward fostering trust that she wasn't trying to gouge someone or pull the wool over their eyes.

Appropriate footwear on, Laine headed out. She knew she probably looked silly, but no one would see her in her skirt, lacy top, and comfortable old boots. She normally wouldn't wear a skirt while touring a property, but she'd had lunch with new clients earlier, and had wanted to look professional.

She slowly circled the house, looking at the foundation, seeing if she noticed signs of termites or other critters, and even checked the wood in places to see if it had rotted away in the heat of the sun and the harsh Texas weather conditions.

As she rounded the side of the house, pleased so far with what she'd seen, Laine stopped dead in her tracks. Sitting in front of the large porch was the ugliest dog she'd ever seen. No, ugly wasn't fair . . . pathetic was a better description.

It had been a long time since the dog had seen

any kind of gentle care. Her fur was filthy. It looked like some sort of pit bull mix. She was obviously female, as her teats hung low, as if she had puppies somewhere who relied on their mother for nourishment. As Laine took a step toward her, the dog's tail tucked between her legs and she backed up.

"Oh, you poor thing. I'm not gonna hurt you. Do you have babies somewhere? I don't blame you for being wary of me. Come here, baby." Laine knelt down in the dirt and held out her hand, trying to coax the dog to her.

When it was obvious the dog wasn't going to come near her, Laine said out loud, more to herself than the dog, "You look hungry. I bet I have something in my car that you'd like."

She stood up and the dog made a break for the barn at her sudden movement, keeping well out of her way.

Laine's heart broke. She wanted to hold the dog and reassure her that she'd never hurt her, but the dog wasn't going to let her get anywhere close.

The house forgotten for a moment, Laine opened her passenger-side door to see what she could scrounge up from her purse. Thankful that she always carried some sort of snack, Laine triumphantly pulled out a granola bar. Luckily, it had no chocolate in it, so the dog could safely eat it. It was some sort of protein thing, which tasted like shit, but Laine didn't think the dog would care. She peeled off the wrapper and dropped it onto her purse to throw away later before she shut the door.

Looking over at the barn, Laine saw the dog peering at her from the broken door. She walked slowly toward the barn, stopping when she was halfway there, figuring any farther would be pushing her luck. She broke the granola bar into pieces and placed them on the ground, knowing the poor dog wouldn't care about a little dirt on the snack.

"There ya go. See? It's just food. I'm sure you're hungry. You look hungry to me. I know it tastes horrible, but you need the fuel. Think of your puppies. They need you to stay healthy, I'm sure." She stepped back slowly, not taking her eyes off the dog. "Go on, it's safe. Promise. I'll stay out of your way while you check it out. It's all yours, I'm not gonna steal it back before you can get it."

Pleased when the dog slunk toward the food, Laine kept backing away. She stayed about twenty feet from the dog the entire time and smiled when she sniffed her offering and then wolfed it down, never taking her eyes from Laine.

Feeling as if she'd won a gold medal in the Olympics when the mangy mutt wagged her tail, Laine smiled and took a step toward her.

Startled anew at her movement, the dog whirled and took off around the side of house.

"Darn." Looking around—for what, Laine had no clue—she shrugged and followed where the dog had gone. There was no one out there. There were a few clumps of trees here and there, but for the most part the land was empty and desolate. There was no way she could just leave the dog and puppies. Even though she hadn't seen any signs of other dogs or of the puppies, there had to be some around. Most likely in the barn. Laine had no idea how she'd get the frightened animal, or any puppies she might find, in her car, but felt she had to try.

Rounding the back of the house, she saw the dog sitting about a hundred yards into a large pasture. She was sitting on her haunches now, as if she didn't have a care in the world. Laine ducked under the rail of an old wooden fence and climbed through after the dog. She spoke to her as she walked, keeping her eyes on her, trying to portray friendly vibes.

"It's okay. I'm not going to hurt you. You look like you need some help. Those mats can't feel good, right? I can bring you to a lady who can shave those things right off. You'll feel two hundred times better once they're gone, promise. And food. Oh, as much as you can eat. Your babies will get the care they need too. You're probably tired of them nursing, yeah? They'll get their own food and you can get healthy again. I don't know what kind of dog you are, but I bet you're beautiful under all that muck, aren't you? I might be able to find something else for you—"

Laine's words were cut off as the ground under her gave way and she screamed, terrified, as she fell. The pain radiating up from her ankles as she landed made her knees immediately buckle, and she fell onto her butt into about half a foot of water. The boards, which had been covering whatever she'd fallen into, bit into her skin and made her groan out in pain as she sat there for a moment trying to process exactly what had just happened.

Laine could feel the darkness creeping in at the sides of her eyes from the pain in her ankles, but she closed her eyes and tried to breathe deeply until the sensation passed. When she thought she was past the danger of fainting, she opened her eyes and looked up, needing to know just what the hell she'd gotten herself into now.

She could see the blue sky and the light fluffy

clouds she'd thought so pretty ten minutes ago above her head . . . *way* above her head. She was probably around twenty feet down, with no way of climbing out. There were no hand holes or steps leading up. She was in some sort of shaft . . . if she had to guess, she thought maybe it was an old well.

It smelled musty, as if it'd been covered up for a long time. Laine sneezed three times in a row as the mold in the air tickled her nose. She put her hand on the side of her tomb to test the strength of the walls surrounding her. The dirt flaked off in her hand. It was more like clay, but Laine could see as the walls went upward, the clay made way to drier dirt. Hell, she was lucky she wasn't buried alive. She knew as well as anyone how dangerous these old wells were. With the droughts they'd had recently, many wells were drying up and even collapsing because of the lack of water in the soil.

Laine half sighed, half sobbed, not believing how stupid she'd been. All of her attention had been on the dog, and not on where she was walking. Laine knew better. She'd been trained on how to recognize the signs of abandoned wells on properties. Had to sit through an entire class for her realtor's license, in fact. Laine thought back to what she'd learned in the eight-hour course . . . pipes sticking up, depressions in the earth, windmills, or random pieces of lumber lying around. They were all signs that there might be a well or mine, and to beware.

Knowing she wasn't going to be able to get out, Laine climbed to her feet carefully, and turned her attention to her immediate surroundings. She was standing in about six inches of black, murky water; luckily it wasn't more. There were some sort of insects on the surface of the water and Laine couldn't help but think of snakes and leeches. Figuring she was safe from snakes, thank God, as she didn't immediately see any, her concern went to the bugs that decided she must've been sent by a higher power to feed them. They were on her legs and buzzing around her face. Laine waved a hand in front of her to try to keep them away.

Her ankles hurt. They'd taken the brunt of the landing from her fall. She cautiously moved one; it throbbed, but she didn't think it was broken. Somehow she must've used her hands to slow her fall on her way down. Whatever the reason, she was glad she wasn't more injured than she was. Laine didn't dare take her boots off to check her ankles, for fear if they started swelling, she'd never get them back on.

The wooden boards lay around her, mocking her

decision to step on them. She shifted and piled them up. When they were stacked, they made somewhat of a seat, which was high enough to be out of the water. It wasn't comfortable, but at least she wouldn't have to have her butt in the water all the time. The diameter of the well was probably around three feet, not huge, but she could turn around. When she sat, her knees had a bit of room, but not a lot. There was certainly no way to lie down. Sleeping wouldn't be something that she'd be doing much of, that was obvious.

Laine shivered. The sunlight wasn't able to reach the bottom of the hole she was in because of the position of the sun, and she was wet from the water she'd landed in when she fell. As her situation sank in, Laine's heart sank with it, and she swallowed the bile that crept up her throat.

She was in deep shit. Her phone was sitting in her car . . . off. When she didn't show up at Wes's, he'd look for her. He was a Texas Ranger, he would use his connections to try to find her. The first thing he'd do was try to track her phone . . . but she'd turned it off to save the stupid battery.

She hadn't told anyone where she was going either. She'd never had reason to in the past. Rose, one of her friends at work, knew she had plans to tour a property, but not which one. Same with Wes. She'd texted him that she'd be at his place later, but she hadn't told one person the address of the ranch. She was a smart, independent woman—who made a dumb mistake not to share the details with anyone as to where she was headed alone. When she made it out, she'd not make that mistake again.

The first tear escaped her eye and Laine tried not to give in to the despair she was feeling. She wiped it away, knowing she was smearing dirt on her face, but not particularly caring at the moment.

Wes would find her. She had to believe that. He always bragged about his success rate with his cases so he wouldn't give up on her. The only question was —would he find her before she died of dehydration or infection or who the hell knew what else?

Laine looked at the water at her feet, trying to determine if it was drinkable. She shivered; it was gross. There were both dead and live bugs floating on top and it looked absolutely disgusting, but Laine knew she'd be drinking it later if she had to. She'd do whatever it took to give Wes, and even Dax, the time they needed to find her. She had no doubt they'd be looking.

Laine wanted to live. She was too young to die.

Hearing a noise, Laine's head whipped up to the

opening of the hole, high above her . . . and she saw the stray dog. She bit back a hysterical laugh. Of course. *Now* the dog was curious. *Now* she came over to see what she was all about.

Resting her head on the dirt wall behind her, not caring in the least about how filthy she was going to be when she was finally hauled out of this tomb in the ground, she refused to think that this would be her final resting place. Laine did what any sane person would do . . . she talked to the dog as if she could understand her.

"Hey there. I'm pretty safe down here now, aren't I? I can't hit you, or kick you . . . or any other number of things, can I? Here's the deal . . . how about you go and get some help. Run to the road, flag down a motorist, preferably a trustworthy one and not a big, scary, hairy guy who would rescue me only to rape and torture me to death. And while I'm asking, make it a cop, would you? You've got all sorts to choose from. Let's see . . . SAPD, maybe a game warden, a sheriff's deputy, FBI or CIA agent, and I'd even take a medical examiner like Calder. Any of them will do. Oh, I know, you can pick a firefighter. If you can get one from Station 7, that'd be great. I've met most of them. Then lead him or her or them back here to this hole in the ground. There's a big juicy steak in it for you if you do."

The dog lay next to the hole and rested her head on her paws as she continued to look down into the deep hole. She didn't make a sound, only watched her with what seemed like curiosity.

The tears began again, and Laine felt her lip quiver as well. She wrapped her arms around her waist and continued to talk out loud. It made her feel better to hear her own voice. Made her feel not so alone. "Where's Lassie when you need him? I'm scared, dog. I fucked up and I'm scared I'm gonna die down here and no one will ever find my body. I need Wes. I'm usually pretty self-reliant, but I'd give anything to have his strong arms around me, telling me it'll all be okay."

The dog didn't answer; only lay at the mouth of the abandoned well as if trying to understand what the strange human was doing.

9

WES PACED the floor in agitation. Laine was late. Very late. Like three hours late. It was nine o'clock already and she was supposed to have been at his place at six. He'd texted and called her cell and gotten no answer. The call had gone straight to voice mail, as if her phone was turned off or dead.

They'd had a conversation about keeping her cell charged, so it could be she'd forgotten to charge it again. But he didn't think so. She'd been very apologetic when he'd explained why he was so upset with her, and seeing him distressed troubled her in return, and she'd sworn she wouldn't let it go dead again. That had only been a week and a half ago, and Wes didn't think she'd break that promise so soon after they'd had the discussion.

Wes had called Dax to see if Mackenzie had heard from her best friend. She hadn't. Dax and Mack had even driven over to Laine's house to see if she was there, and Mack had used her key to go inside to make sure she wasn't injured and not able to get to the door . . . but neither she nor her car were there and it didn't look like she'd been home that night after work.

The last thing Laine had told him via text was that she was going to check out a property.

All sorts of horrible scenarios ran through Wes's head. He couldn't turn off his Ranger brain, thinking about all of the scary things that could've happened to her. Someone could've followed her and accosted her while she was isolated. She could've gotten in a car accident. She could be lost, although that was unlikely since she had a map app on her phone.

She could simply be doing some errands and running late. But in the past, when she'd been running late, she'd called or texted him. He didn't want to embarrass her if nothing was wrong, but he was worried.

Deciding he'd waited long enough, Wes decided it was time to call in the cavalry.

Wes didn't have a close contact with anyone in the SAPD, so he called their general line. His position as a Texas Ranger went a long way toward getting him immediate attention and accelerating the investigation. Typically, people had to be missing for at least twenty-four hours before a report could be taken and the wheels of an investigation started, but thankfully in this case, things were moving quickly.

When Dax had heard about Wes's concerns, he'd called his friend, Cruz, in the FBI, as well as another friend, Lieutenant Quint Axton, who Wes didn't know, in the SAPD. It was all very confusing and Wes wasn't even sure how Dax was connected to everyone, but when Hayden Yates, from the Sheriff's Department, had called and said that Fire Station 7 had their paramedics on standby, just in case, and to let her know if she could do anything, he gave up trying to figure it out, relieved that at least things were happening quickly.

He'd seen his brothers and sisters in blue . . . and red . . . in action in the past, rallying around their own when they were in trouble, but he'd never had to rely on them for his own personal use before. But Wes knew he needed every single eye, every single brain, to figure out where Laine was. He was well aware that the first twenty-four hours of any missing persons case was critical. If Laine had been kidnapped, it was likely the person would either kill her outright, or would keep her to . . . do whatever . . . to her for at least a few hours. It was that "whatever" that Wes didn't want to think about.

He and Laine had been dating, and even though he saw the bad things that could happen to people, and even the awful things that humans could do to each other, through the course of his job, he still hadn't really thought anything would happen to either of *them*. They'd been enjoying getting to know each other, in and out of the bedroom. She was quickly becoming one of his best friends, which felt right. Wes never thought he'd lose her, not so soon after he'd found her, or that there might be a chance she'd disappear from his life in such a mysterious way.

He had a new respect and empathy for the families of missing persons he'd spoken to in the past. He'd felt bad for them, but hadn't really understood what they were going through . . . until now.

As Wes stood in his house, clutching his phone, willing Laine to call him and tell him with that nervous laugh she had that it was all a misunderstanding, it hit him.

He loved her.

He was devastated just *thinking* about never

seeing her again. If she really was gone, he suddenly realized he would've lost one of the best things that had ever happened to him. He might've been telling himself they were just dating, but it was suddenly very obvious that wasn't the case.

He hadn't told her, they hadn't spoken of love to each other, but it was there nonetheless. Wes figured he'd loved her from the first time he saw her standing in his barn. From her nipple hard-ons, as she called them, to the blush on her face when she realized she'd been staring at him, he loved everything about her. She was his soul mate—and he didn't even want to think about how he might not get the chance to tell her.

As the night wore on, and his adrenaline spiked each time the phone rang, then plummeted when he realized it wasn't Laine on the other end, Wes's determination hardened. She was out there . . . somewhere. He'd spent his entire life investigating crimes and murders and missing persons. He was going to have to use every ounce of what he'd learned over the years in law enforcement to track her down. Somehow he knew Laine was waiting for him, counting on him to do his job and find her.

It was almost as if he could hear her words in his ear . . . whispering over and over, "Find me, Wes. I'm waiting for you to figure out what happened and come get me."

LAINE SHIVERED in the narrow space, but kept her chin tilted up so she could see the sky. Seeing proof she wasn't buried alive kept the claustrophobia she was feeling at bay . . . for now. The night was clear and the stars out here in the middle of nowhere were shining just as bright as they were on her first date with Wes. Looking up at the same stars she'd gazed at with Wes made her feel closer to him. Was he out there right this second, looking up at the sky and thinking about her? If so, they were seeing the same stars . . . somehow that felt significant to her.

"I wonder if there are aliens out there, dog," she croaked out in a hoarse voice. She'd been talking to the dog for hours; it made her feel not quite so alone. "Maybe ET is out there now, lying on his back looking up at his purple sky and three moons and wondering what happened to his little friend he left behind on Earth."

The dog had been gone a while, but Laine kept speaking to her, nevertheless. She knew the mutt was probably gone for good . . . off to take care of her puppies, or to find something to eat. She certainly had no reason to continue to hang out at the top of a hole and stare down at her. She really wasn't that exciting.

Laine shuddered again and wrapped her arms around her waist even tighter. She'd tried to prop her heels up on the boards by her butt and pull her skirt over her bare legs to keep warm, but it didn't work. The boards were too short and her ankles throbbed when she kept them in that position too long. She was covered in bug bites, the mosquitos having a field day with her fresh blood. Laine had resorted to using the water to wet the dirt on the walls to smear all over her arms and legs. It was drying now, and she felt like an experiment at the spa gone wrong.

Thinking back to the missing dog, Laine knew that even though it was Texas, it was chilly in the fall at night, and the dog was probably curled around her babies, snug and warm, the strange human a long-forgotten memory.

"Maybe if I send up a quick prayer, a cyborg or alien will hear it in passing and send down a search team. They'll find me in this hole and beam me up, like on *Star Trek*. They'll fix up my ankles, and put me in that beautiful blue dress that Cinderella wore in the latest version of the movie. I'll twirl around and around and when I stop, Wes will be there in his Ranger uniform. He'll tip his Stetson to me and we'll dance off into the sunset."

When she stopped talking, Laine couldn't hear a thing other than the crickets and their incessant chirping. "Oh my God," she exclaimed to the night. "I really *have* turned into Mackenzie. Seriously, this is too much. I've made fun of her my entire life for babbling on and on, but look at me. I'm doing the same damn thing."

Laine closed her eyes and her chin fell to her chest in despair. Her words came out as a whisper this time, "I need you, Wes. Please, don't stop looking for me. I'm here. I'm right here."

AT SEVEN O'CLOCK the next morning, Wes met Rose, a realtor who worked with Laine, at their office. She showed him Laine's cubicle, and he got to work going through her files. He wasn't a computer geek, so he was out of luck on searching her computer, not able to even log in because he didn't know her password, but lucky for him, Laine was old school. She had a calendar sitting on her desk with doodles and appointments all over it. He found a drawer full of papers about various listings and notes on houses in the area.

It took him three hours to go through it all, but just when he was about to give up, he thought he just might have found a clue. On yesterday's date, she'd written, "Johnson." It was, unfortunately, a common name, but she'd also scribbled "Morningside."

Doing a quick Google search on his phone, Wes found that there was a Morningside Long-Term Care Facility in the city. The two weren't necessarily connected, but it was more than he had before he'd been to her office. He quickly dialed the number on their website.

"Good morning, Morningside Long-Term Care, where we care for your loved one as much as you do. How can I help you?"

"My name is Westin King. I'm a Texas Ranger investigating a missing persons case."

"Oh, how can I help you?" the lady on the other end of the line repeated, sounding more concerned rather than falsely chipper, as she had when she'd answered.

"Do you have any patients with the last name of

Johnson?" As soon as he asked the question, he knew he was being too vague.

"Yes. But none of them are missing."

"Let me be more specific. The woman who has disappeared is a realtor. The last time anyone heard from her, she was going to look at a property. We don't know where the property is, or even whose it was. The only clue we have is the last name of Johnson written on her calendar yesterday, with Morningside written on the same date. I was hoping you might know of anyone who might be in your facility who's putting their house up for sale? Or maybe their relatives are?" Wes knew he sounded desperate, but he couldn't help it.

"I'm really sorry, I'm just the front desk person. I have a list of our patients, but I'm not close enough to them to know about their personal lives."

Wes gritted his teeth, knowing every second that went by was a second that Laine needed him, and he wasn't there for her. "Can you please ask around and call me back as soon as you can? The woman who's missing is my girlfriend. This is personal for me. Please. Anything you might be able to find out could mean the difference between life and death for her."

The sympathy Wes heard in the woman's voice, even over the phone, was palpable. "Of course. We can't tell you any medical information or anything, but I'll check the patient list and see if I can talk to the nurses who work with anyone with the last name of Johnson. Maybe they'll know more."

"Thank you." Wes gave the woman his number and clicked off the phone and tried to think. He'd asked Dax's friend in the FBI, Cruz, to use his connections to trace Laine's cell phone, but that hadn't exactly been the home run they'd needed. The phone was now either turned off, dead, or destroyed. They had no way to tell, but the bottom line was that it wasn't transmitting a signal, so it couldn't be traced.

Cruz's FBI tech contact had been able to tell him that it had last pinged at a tower south of the city, but the area was very rural, and there was no guarantee she was anywhere near there now. Wes wanted more information before he organized a huge search party of the area, which might end up being a waste of time. He needed to narrow it down, or at least have more concrete evidence on where she might be first.

His phone rang and Wes put it up to his ear after clicking the green talk button. "King here."

"Have you found her?" Mack's frantic voice echoed though his brain.

"No."

"Where could she be? Daxton and I drove around a bit last night looking for her, with no luck. Cruz and Mickie got together with Calder and Hayden and searched around her house. No one they talked to had seen her. Even the guys who weren't on duty at the fire station were out looking. Where's her car? If we find her car, I bet we'll find her. She has to be somewhere, Wes! Dammit! Where is she?"

Wes didn't get upset at Mackenzie. He'd been around her enough in the last month or so to know how she was. She wasn't accusing him and was obviously just as worried as he was about Laine. "I don't know. But I'm following up on a lead. I'm going to find her. There's no way I've gone forty-two years before finding my soul mate to lose her now."

When Mack didn't say anything, Wes said, "Mackenzie?"

Then he heard her sob. Shit. Dax's voice came over the line.

"What? Did you find her? Is she hurt?"

"I haven't found her, Dax."

"Then why is Mack crying?"

"Because I basically told her how much I love her friend. Because she's emotional. Because she wants to find her friend as much as I do." His voice dropped in anguish. "Because I have no fucking idea where Laine is and it's tearing me apart."

"Dammit, Wes. This doesn't make sense. Any leads on the BOLO?"

Wes appreciated his friend not commenting on his break in professionalism, instead focusing on the "Be On The Lookout" Wes had put on Laine's car. He cleared his throat, got himself under control and answered. "No. Nothing. But that's not too surprising. If it's parked amongst other cars or otherwise doesn't stick out, it could take days or weeks to find."

They both knew her car could be anywhere. It could be at the bottom of a pond or lake . . . with Laine still inside. If she'd crashed, it could be years before anyone found it, or her. Or the car, and Laine, could be in Mexico . . . or another state. There were so many scary scenarios, it hurt Wes's heart to even think about what may have happened to her.

"I called in a favor from a friend of a friend of a friend," Dax told Wes in a serious voice. "Moose is a firefighter from Station 7 that I've worked with in the past. As you know, we've played Station 7 in those charity softball games for several years now. Anyway, one of his crew is the Army Princess—"

"The soldier who was rescued from the Middle East? The one held by ISIS?" Wes interrupted in surprise. He'd met the firefighters, but wasn't close with them. But now that he thought about it, Penelope, the female firefighter, did look familiar. He vaguely remembered all the press coverage on her when she'd been held as a prisoner over in Turkey.

"Yes, that's her. Anyway, somehow in all that went down with her, she met this man who's a former SEAL and some sort of techy geek. Penelope heard from Moose that Laine was missing, and she knows she's Mack's best friend, and since Mack is my girlfriend . . . shit, it's all so convoluted, but anyway, the bottom line is that this guy did some searching to try to help . . . and he came up blank."

"What?" Wes asked in surprise, sure Dax had been about to tell him that this mysterious hacker had found Laine.

"Yeah, I think it stunned him as much as it did us. He told us the same thing Cruz's guy did about the phone. He knows it pinged on that rural tower, but that doesn't give us enough information to organize a search party or head down there to start looking in any constructive way. He couldn't find any local surveillance cameras with her car or license on it. He's been up most of the night searching databases, with no luck. He says that he could probably find her if he had more time and information, but we're running low on both at the moment. I'm kinda at a loss."

Wes knew the connection between Laine and this mysterious guy was tenuous at best, but he wouldn't look a gift horse in the mouth. "Ask him to look into a property owned by someone with the last name of Johnson in that area. Also, Morningside. Both names were written on yesterday's date on the calendar at Laine's desk. I've searched through all of the MLS listings in her files, without success. I'm waiting on a call back from someone at a long-term care facility named Morningside, here in San Antonio, but I have no idea when they'll get back to me, or if anyone will have anything that will be useful enough to find Laine. We know she was looking at a property, but not where or whose. I'm hoping this mysterious property owned by someone with the last name of Johnson was where she disappeared. If not . . . I have no idea where to go next."

"Will do. Let me see if I can get Moose to ask Penelope to contact him again. Jesus . . . this feels like the telephone game," Dax said in disgust.

"Give him my number. He can call me direct," Wes demanded, thinking much like Dax, that they needed to cut out the middlemen.

"I will. Don't give up, Wes. Remember, we found

Mack when all the odds were against it. Laine comes from the same stock as Mack. She's tough and I know we'll find her."

"I know. Thanks, Dax. I appreciate it."

"Anytime. Not only because you're my friend, but because if anything happens to Laine, it'll devastate Mack."

"She still there?"

"No, I sent her to the other room to lie down. She didn't sleep at all last night and she's stressed out to her breaking point."

"Take care of her. I've come to like that woman of yours."

"I will. Call me the second you have a lead. I've got a whole team of people ready to move at a moment's notice. Firefighters, cops, paramedics . . . you name it."

Not for the first time, Wes thanked his lucky stars he was where he was and he'd made the type of friends he had. It was as if Fate had made him wait as long as she did to find the woman meant for him, until he had exactly the right combination of friends around him. If anyone could find and save Laine, it was the army of law enforcement and firefighter friends who were on his side. "I will. Thank you.

Seriously, you have no idea how much that means to me. I'll be in touch."

"It's what Rangers do. And friends, Wes. Later."

"Later."

Wes was striding toward the front of the building before he'd finished speaking. He couldn't just sit around and wait for a phone call. He didn't know what he needed to do, but waiting idly was at the bottom of the list.

10

THE DOG WAS BACK. Laine looked up and saw her muzzle peeking over the edge of the hole, way above her head. "Hey, dog. You come back to laugh at me some more?" Sometime in the last two days, Laine decided that was really what the dog was doing. She was obviously wary of people and was probably thinking karma was getting back at the human race.

The first night hadn't been so bad . . . she'd been sure Wes, or Dax, or someone would realize she was missing and track her down, and she'd be sitting at Wes's house eating breakfast within hours. But as the second day came and went, she understood the trouble she was in.

Laine was thirsty. She couldn't remember exactly how long it was before someone died from a lack of water, but she thought she could probably hold out a few more days. The fact that she was thinking about how many *days* she might have to live was absolutely terrifying.

She'd stopped sweating the day before and she was dizzy most of the time now. Her mouth felt as though she'd been sucking on cotton balls, but it was the confusion that scared her most of all. Laine had woken up a while ago and had no idea where she was. She'd stood up and tried to take a step and ran her face into the dirt wall. She'd fallen on her butt on the boards and it'd taken her too many minutes to work through in her mind where she was and how she'd gotten there. She was terrified that her body was shutting down on her.

Her voice was still scratchy, but along with the chills, hunger, thirst, and all of her aches and pains, Laine could add shaking to her list of things that were just not going her way.

"You run off to get help yet?" she asked the dog, still staring down at her. "'Cos I could really use some here." Laine stood for a moment, and wished with all her heart she could lay down. The first night had been long, cold, and uncomfortable, but the second had been absolute misery. Her legs were cramping and her back was killing her from not being able to stretch it out properly. The bruises from her initial decent into hell were starting to make themselves known as well. She'd slept in spurts, sitting up. Her neck hurt, but not as much as her ankles. She'd started trying to stand for periods of time, ignoring the shooting pains in her legs. If she got a blood clot from sitting for too long, she'd die of that as easily as anything else.

Once, when she was completely miserable, she'd given climbing the walls of the abandoned well the ol' college try, and failed miserably. All she'd done was make her ankles ache more, and rip a large chunk of dirt from the wall of the shaft, further contaminating the murky water at her feet. She had to look like the monster from the black lagoon by now. Covered in dried mud from her attempts at using it for a bug repellant, and the additional dirt and mud that she'd gotten on her over the last forty hours or so.

The water had finally begun to seep through the weathered leather of her boots and Laine could feel her toes squishing in her socks. And she was thirsty. So damn thirsty. Now that the sun had come up again, the temperature had risen in her hole. It wasn't as bad as it could've been if she'd been in direct sunlight, or if it'd been the middle of summer, but the gnats and other insects had taken up residence with her again and were driving her crazy, along with all her other maladies.

The dog panted as she whined above her. "Now I know how you felt when I got here, girl. I hope that granola bar was good. I'd kill for one, although it'd make me even thirstier than I am now, which would totally suck. You see anyone up there? Anyone at all? Maybe someone will come look at this stupid house. It is on the market, after all. I know, I know," Laine continued the one-sided conversation, not expecting the dog to suddenly talk back, "it's been on the market for two years and hasn't had one contract on it . . . but you never know. Maybe today's the day. Maybe today, someone will decide they want to live on a real live ranch and take a tour."

Laine eased herself back to her makeshift seat on the rotten boards and fell silent. She was cried out, and didn't have any tears anymore anyway. She closed her eyes, feeling tired. So tired. She'd just close her eyes for a moment; she'd be okay, she was just resting her eyeballs.

As she fell into a fitful sleep, she didn't even notice the gnats settling on her face, or that the dog stayed by the hole high above her head, as if watching over her.

WES TRIED to look around Laine's house with the eye of a detective, rather than the man who recently had an epiphany that he loved her. The first night had been bad, but he'd still held out hope that she was hunkered down somewhere and not really missing, but now that a second night had come and gone with no word from or about her, the feeling in his gut that she would die if he didn't locate her was eating away at him.

Dax's mysterious techie friend hadn't called him back yet, neither had anyone from Morningside, and he'd taken to driving the streets of San Antonio, trying to see if he could find Laine's car. In a last-ditch effort, he'd gone to visit Dax and Mack and had gotten the key to her apartment from Mackenzie, wanting to see for himself that she hadn't come home and packed to go on a spur-of-the-moment trip or something.

Not being able to find her, and not having any information coming in, was killing him. He should've found her by now. He felt like he was on the cusp of having all the information they needed, but hadn't been able to put the pieces together. It was incredibly frustrating.

Everything at Laine's house looked in place, exactly as it'd been the last time he'd seen Laine. Nothing was knocked over, as if she'd been in a tussle with someone. Her boots and sandals were missing, which wasn't unusual, she usually had the boots in her car in case she needed to walk around a muddy or dangerous property. There wasn't any food left out on the counter. It was exactly as if she'd gotten ready for a day of work with every intention of returning. Dammit.

His phone rang, and Wes answered immediately with a terse, "King."

"My name is Tex, and I'm the friend of a friend of a friend who's been looking into your missing girl-friend." The man on the other end of the phone didn't bother beating around the bush.

Wes didn't care about introductions at this point, he was just glad to finally be hearing from Dax's friend. "Do you have anything?"

"Yes. I'm pretty sure I do. You were right on, and I don't think I would've found what I did without your help. I searched the MLS database for a property for sale by someone with the last name of Johnson. There were four hundred and thirty-two in and around San Antonio."

Wes's stomach dropped, but he didn't get a chance to say anything as Tex continued.

"But there's only one that's connected to Morningside Long-Term Care Facility *and* is south of the city. Ethel Johnson, age ninety-two. She's been there for four years. She has one daughter, who lives up in Austin. The ranch went on the market two years ago and the price has dropped three times. They own it outright, so there's no mortgage. I took the liberty of hacking into one of the government's satellites and checking it out with the best cameras available. Not that crap that Google uses. According to the DMV, Laine owns a 2012 Toyota Avalon. It's hard to be one hundred percent sure, but it looks like there's an Avalon sitting in front of the house at the property in question."

Wes didn't give a shit at the moment how many laws the man on the other end of the phone had just broken, or about the fact that he'd admitted as much to a law enforcement officer. All he cared about was Laine, and it looked like he was finally getting a viable lead. Sometimes it worked that way in his job. He'd work for days with nothing, and the most inconsequential thing could lead to solving the case.

"What's the address?" Wes's heart rate increased. He'd known it.

Tex gave it to him then warned, "I've already told Penelope, who's most likely informed the rest of her crew and Mackenzie by now. I'm sure *she's* told Daxton, so if you're heading out there, be ready for the cavalry to be at your heels."

"If she's there, I'm forever in your debt."

"No, you aren't. You'd do the same if it was my wife. And you have, not with me or mine, but with many, many other people. I've looked into your record. You're a hell of a Ranger. It's my honor to help you. Let me know if you ever need any other help. I've got your back, King. Good luck and godspeed."

Wes didn't bother saying goodbye, as the other man had already hung up. He closed and locked Laine's apartment door behind him and climbed into his vehicle, taking the extra seconds to put the address Tex had given him into his GPS. It sucked to take the time, but it would be even worse to be lost on the back roads of southern Texas, knowing he was close to Laine, but not getting there in time because he'd been a dumbass.

As he raced to the deserted ranch, his phone rang once again. Expecting it to be Dax or one of his other fellow Rangers, Wes answered brusquely, "Yeah?"

"Is this Texas Ranger Wes King?" The voice was hesitant after hearing the sharp way he'd answered.

"Sorry, yes, this is he. Can I help you?"

"My name is Mary. I work at Morningside. Our receptionist said you were interested in one of our patients with the last name of Johnson that was maybe selling a house?"

Wes was pretty sure he had the information he needed already, but he didn't tell Mary that. "Yes, do you know of anyone like that?"

"Yes. Ethel Johnson is in her nineties and the sweetest woman I know. I've spent many a night sitting up with her listening to the stories of her life in that house. Her husband died twenty years ago and she's been lonely ever since. Her daughter tried to help as much as she could, but since she lives in Austin, she couldn't be around all the time. A few years ago, Ethel fell and couldn't get up. Her daughter decided she needed to be in an assisted-living facility, and she's been here ever since."

"Can you tell me the address?"

"No, I'm sorry. I would if I could, but I don't know it. But I *do* know it was south of the city. Ethel sometimes talks about how she and her husband used to sit on the roof and gaze northward at the city lights."

Tex had been right. He was on the right track.

The address he was racing toward *was* south of San Antonio. Wes was relieved, but not a hundred percent. He might have the address of the property Laine was going to look at, but that didn't mean she was there. But at least it was a place to start. "Thank you, Mary, I appreciate you calling me back."

"Do you think the missing woman might be out there?"

"I don't know, but I'm praying she is."

"Good luck. I hope she's okay."

"Me too. Please tell Ethel she'll have a visitor soon. I'd like to come and thank her myself once I find my girlfriend."

"Oh, she'll like that. Will you wear your uniform? She has a thing for cowboy hats, *and* the cowboys who wear them."

"I will. Thanks again."

"Bye, Ranger."

Wes clicked off the Bluetooth on his phone and gripped the steering wheel hard as he raced south. "Hold on, Laine, I'm coming for you." His words were whispered, but he hoped with all his heart that the man upstairs was listening and would keep the woman he loved safe until he could get there.

11

WES DROVE down the rutted and badly in-need-of-repair dirt and gravel driveway at a speed much too fast than was safe, but he didn't care. Turning one last corner, he saw a house—but more importantly, Laine's car.

Daxton was already there, leaning into the driver's side.

Not bothering to pull the keys out of the ignition, Wes slammed his car into park and jumped out.

"What do you have?" he growled out at his friend in agitation.

"Nothing. Her keys aren't here. But her purse is. Her phone is in it."

Wes walked around to the other side of the Avalon and opened the door. Her purse was sitting on the passenger seat, with a granola bar wrapper and her phone resting on top, as if she'd thrown both there without much worry. It didn't look like anything was out of the ordinary with the car. The seat looked to be in the right position for her five-nine height. There was no blood or anything else that would be evidence of a struggle.

Using his shirt to pick up her phone, trying to preserve evidence if it was needed later, Wes turned it on. The charge was at twelve percent. "It's almost dead. I bet she turned it off to try to conserve it. We had a conversation about it and she was probably trying to make sure it didn't die altogether."

Dax nodded in agreement. "Her sandals are on the floorboard near the pedals. She took the time to change into her boots. It doesn't look like she was in distress, at least when she left her car."

They both looked around the car and could see Laine's footprints all over the dusty ground. They led toward the house as well as partway to the barn. They weren't spaced far enough apart for her to be running. She was just walking around. They didn't immediately see any other footprints indicating another person had been there and had possibly snatched Laine, but somehow it didn't make Wes feel better. She was still missing.

He looked around at the desolate property and the hair on his arms stood up. Laine was close. He could feel it.

Before they could split up to begin searching for her, a line of cars made their way up the long driveway. All of Dax's friends piled out. Quint, Hayden, Cruz, Calder, TJ, and even Conor, came up to them.

An ambulance bounced along the driveway next, as well as a brush truck from Station 7. A short woman who Wes now recognized as the infamous Penelope Turner, the Army Princess herself, popped out, along with five other firemen. Even though he'd met them in passing before, they were quickly re-introduced as Moose, Sledge, Chief, Squirrel, and Driftwood.

"Taco and Crash had to stay back in case we got any calls, and they're pissed. But they said if we needed anything, to call it in and they'd send anyone and everyone they could," the tall firefighter named Moose explained to the group.

Wes wasn't sure who Taco and Crash were, but he didn't care. He was feeling extremely emotional at the moment, thankful for the support of so many wonderful men and women.

He swallowed the knot in his throat and quickly organized a search. "Okay, everyone pair up. A firefighter with a cop. Don't be a hero. If you find her, call out, but be careful. We have no idea what the structural integrities of the buildings are. There might be a bad guy hiding out. The last thing we want is a shoot-out or a hostage situation. Be smart, stay alert. If you find anything, don't touch it. If there are fingerprints, we need to preserve them. Look down, you can see her footprints. She's wearing boots. Don't mess them up, if you can help it. They could help later. If you find, Laine," Wes's voice cracked, but he choked it down and continued with determination, "call out or whistle so the rest of us can get there to help. Any questions?"

When no one said a word, they all spread out, watching where they were walking, trying not to obliterate Laine's footsteps as they went.

Dax stayed with Wes as the other pairs headed out. Some went toward the barn, others toward the house. Squirrel and Calder headed up the driveway, looking for clues, and TJ and Driftwood walked around the back of the barn.

Neither Wes nor Dax said a word as they started around the house, following Laine's footprints. Noticing as she stopped here and there to look at the foundation or a gutter that was barely hanging on to the side of the house. They got all the way back around the house and hadn't found any sign of Laine.

Wes stopped and turned in a circle, looking for .. . something. He wasn't sure what, but his gut was screaming at him that they were missing something vital.

"What is it?" Dax asked, standing patiently by his side.

"I don't know. I'm trying to see this place through her eyes." They heard the other pairs of first responders talking to each other as they searched the house. Dax looked over to the barn and saw Quint and Moose coming out. Each was holding two puppies in their arms.

That was it. What was niggling at him finally clicked in his brain. He immediately went around to the back of the house again, knowing Dax followed him. Wes's eyes moved to the large pasture at the back side of the property. He'd glanced at it as they'd rounded the house the first time, but hadn't bothered to pay much attention, more concerned about watching Laine's footprints in the dirt.

He saw what had caught his attention, but hadn't really registered as anything important at the time. A dog.

The dog was sitting in the middle of the field,

motionless. It was odd behavior for any dog . . . friendly or not. She should be either running toward them, if she was friendly, or away from them if she wasn't. And the fact that there were puppies in the barn meant that the dog should be trying to protect them. But she wasn't doing any of that. She was simply sitting on her haunches, head tilted, watching them.

He never would've looked twice in the large field if it wasn't for that dog. Nothing seemed out of place. It was simply a large, flat, open space, full of weeds.

Wes started for the wooden fence, not taking his eyes off the stray that seemed to be watching him with just as much intensity. He heard Dax following him and whistling for Squirrel and the other paramedics to be on standby.

The dog fidgeted a bit as Wes came closer, but didn't bolt. She was a mangy thing . . . had obviously been on her own out at the property for quite a while. She looked skinny, and had scars on her muzzle, as if she'd been in too many fights with other animals to count, but her teats were full of milk and almost dragging the ground, even as she sat still, observing him. Her fur was almost black with dirt. The dog looked extremely pathetic. But Wes didn't care about any of that.

It was the hole the dog was sitting in front of that concerned him the most. He didn't see it until he was almost on top of it.

"Easy. We're not gonna hurt you. Is Laine there? Is that why you're here? You guarding her? You're a good dog. Take it easy."

The dog half whined and half growled low in her throat and backed up as Wes continued his slow, cautious approach. "Keep the others back," Wes warned Dax as he heard the group gathering behind him.

He spoke in a calming voice as he eased to his knees about five feet from the dog . . . and the hole behind her. "She's down there, isn't she? Thank you for watching over her, for staying with her. I bet she was scared, wasn't she? I swear to God, you and your pups have a home for life with me if she's down there. I'll feed you steak every night if you want . . . although just a warning, that might make you get fat."

The dog cocked its head at Wes and her ears perked forward, as if she understood his words.

"Please don't run away, but can I see? Will you let me come closer so I can see if Laine's okay?"

Amazingly, the dog backed up and went to the other side of the jagged hole in the ground. She lay down with her muzzle resting on her paws, never taking her eyes off Wes.

"Thank you," he told the dog earnestly, putting his Stetson to the side and laying on his belly. Wes crept forward, using his elbows and knees to propel him, not knowing how stable the hole in the ground was. Old wells and mines were notorious for caving in if caution wasn't taken. The ground around it seemed solid, but knowing he was most likely this close to Laine made him not want to take any chances.

Wes eased toward the hole, not daring to breathe as he finally got close enough to look down. He couldn't see all the way to the bottom of the cavernous hole. "Give me a flashlight," he ordered, holding his hand back toward the others. Someone, Wes had no idea who, put a light in his palm and he brought it up and clicked it on.

Shining it down into the dark hole, Wes felt the bile crawl up his throat.

He'd found Laine, but he couldn't tell if he was too late or not.

12

LAINE'S HEAD was lying at an awkward angle and Wes could only see the top of it. She was covered in dirt and mud so he couldn't tell if she was bleeding from anywhere. Her legs were splayed apart, her skirt sitting at the tops of her knees. Her frilly blouse was ripped on one shoulder and her arms were hanging limply at her sides. The water in the bottom of the hole reflected back up at him from the light he shone downward. Most importantly and disconcerting, however, was that she wasn't moving.

"Laine? Can you hear me, darlin'?"

"Is she there? How far down is she?"

Wes thought it was Conor who asked.

Without moving from the side of the hole, Wes twisted his head and answered, "Yeah. She's here. I'm not sure, but I think she's about twenty feet down or so. She's hurt, though. I can't tell how badly and she's not answering me." He turned back, heartsick.

"Laine, I'm here. I'm gonna get you out of there. You hear me? Just hang on, I'm coming for you." With one last look at the woman who held his heart in her hand, he scooted back, needing to make a plan.

Wes saw four of the firefighters running toward the house and their truck, hopefully going to get supplies to get Laine out of the hole. Thank God they'd brought their truck. They'd have extraction equipment appropriate for this sort of rescue.

"What did you see?" Conor asked urgently.

"She's sitting at the bottom; again, I think it's about twenty to twenty-five feet down. There's water at the bottom, it reflected off my light, but I can't tell how deep it is. Her head was down, so I didn't get a look at her face. She has to be hurt though. By the looks of the broken boards up here, she most likely stepped on them without even knowing and fell through. I don't know if her neck is broken, or her back or what." Wes tried to keep his voice matter-of-fact, but it took everything he had.

"What was she doing out here in this field?" Penelope asked.

"I don't know, but at the moment, I don't really care," Wes told her, dismissing the question, but not harshly. At this point, it didn't matter if she was running away from someone, or if she'd been out for a little stroll to hunt for chupacabras. What mattered was getting her out and to the hospital and making sure she was okay. They'd deal with all the other stuff later.

Hopefully there'd *be* a later.

Wes and the others continued to strategize as they waited impatiently for the firefighters to make it back to them with their emergency equipment.

Laine groaned softly as she regained consciousness. She knew she was going in and out, but this time seemed different, she was hearing things. "Great, now I'm hallucinating," she tried to say, but all that came out was a faint croak. She opened her eyes and looked up, not sure what she hoped to see. But the sight that greeted her was the same thing she'd seen every time she'd opened her eyes since the sun had risen—the scruffy dog blinking down at her from high above.

She tried to swallow, but her mouth was completely dry and she had nothing *to* swallow. "Hey, mutt, what's new?" Laine whispered, shocked as hell when the dog let out a bark. It was the first time she'd heard the animal make any kind of noise except for a couple of whines when she'd first seen it.

Wes turned in surprise at the sound of the dog's bark. He'd been deep in conversation with the others about the best way to go about getting Laine out of the hole, especially if she had a spinal injury. The mutt was sitting up with her tongue out, panting. She looked at him and barked, then dropped down onto her belly and barked down into the hole.

Without thinking, Wes dropped onto his own stomach and inched his way back to the side of the hole. He felt someone grab hold of his ankles, just in case the hole opened up and collapsed under him. The last thing they needed was him falling into the well on top of Laine.

Peering over the edge, Wes shone the flashlight down into the darkness and almost stopped breathing at the sight that greeted him. Laine was awake and he could see the whites of her eyes in the darkness of the well. "Hey, darlin'." It wasn't what he'd planned to say, but the words popped out anyway.

"Wes? Did that mangy mutt actually pull a Lassie, or am I still hallucinating?" It didn't sound like her, but she managed to get the words out as best she could.

"Not only am I here, but everyone else is too."

"Everyone else?"

Wes winced at the sound of her voice. It was scratchy and he had to strain to hear her, but she was alive and talking, so it was the sweetest sound he'd ever heard.

"Yeah, Dax, Hayden, Cruz, Calder, TJ, Quint, Conor, and most of the crew from Station 7. Are you hurt?"

"Yeah."

When she didn't elaborate, Wes urged her to continue. "Okay, don't move, keep as still as you can. Where, darlin'? Where do you hurt?"

"My ankles. My arms where the planks scratched them. My stomach 'cos it's empty. My feet; they're soaked and probably permanently wrinkled. I've probably lost a size or two off them as a result, Mack might be happy to go shoe shopping with me. My head is pounding, probably because I'm so thirsty, but I refused to drink the sludge in the bottom of this hellhole, but if you'd taken any longer I might've resorted to it. I'm dizzy and my tongue feels like it's three sizes too big."

Her words sounded like they were coming from a

ninety-year-old who smoked a pack of cigarettes a day, but they were understandable, and she was alive. Wes would take it.

"Wow, she sounds an awful lot like Mack right about now," Quint said from behind him. Wes had no idea how they could hear Laine with her voice the way it was, but that didn't matter at the moment. Reassuring the woman he loved did.

"There's an IV up here with your name all over it, Laine. Fresh, clean water all for you. Just hang on, as soon as we get you out of there and hook you up, you'll be needing to pee before you know it."

Laine giggled, and even though it was weak, it was still the sweetest sound Wes had heard in a long time. Just then, Chief and the other three firefighters arrived back from the brush truck and ambulance parked in front of the house. Wes glanced back and saw they had a ladder, as well as rope, a stretcher, a huge first-aid kit, and other rescue paraphernalia.

"Wes, back up. We're gonna hook Squirrel up and lower him down."

"No, I'll go down and get her," Wes argued resolutely.

"You won't fit," Dax told him firmly. "Look at Squirrel, Wes. He's tall and skinny and will be able to fit down there without an issue. He'll hold Laine to him in the harness as we haul them up. You're big; it'll be a better fit with Squirrel."

"Wes?" Laine's voice was still weak, but she'd obviously overheard the conversation.

"Yeah, darlin'?"

"Please let them get me out of here. I've had about enough of this place."

"Do it," Wes told Dax and Squirrel with no more questions. He scooted around to the other side of the hole, not willing to lose sight of Laine. Amazingly, the dog stayed where she was, only moving over a bit, as if giving Wes room.

The entire rescue took no more than ten minutes from start to finish. Squirrel was hooked up to the rappelling gear and was slowly lowered down into the abandoned well. Wes lost sight of Laine as soon as Squirrel blocked the passageway, but he still didn't move. Finally, the firefighter's head appeared at the mouth of the hole after the others pulled both Laine and him up and out.

Squirrel lay on his back and held Laine tightly to his chest, keeping her immobile as his crew tugged him backward and away from the hole. Wes shuffled alongside them, keeping his hand on Laine's back as they moved, needing the physical contact with her.

When they were safely out of the way, Wes let

Moose take hold of Laine's head and hold her neck still as the others assisted in rolling her off Squirrel and onto the waiting stretcher, but he immediately grabbed her hand.

Her eyes were closed, and she looked serene, but her grip on his hand belied her peaceful demeanor. She was covered in dirt from head to toe. Mud was smeared on her legs and arms, her frilly pink blouse was now a dirty brown and her hair was caked with it.

Wes's eyes never strayed from her face as the firefighters worked around them, securing her to the backboard for the trip to the ambulance. She lifted her eyelids when she was finally safely strapped down. The whites of her eyes looked extremely bright against the mud covering her face and hair.

"You sure are a sight for sore eyes, darlin'," Wes whispered into her ear before Moose fit a C-collar on her.

"You have no idea how wonderful it feels to be flat on my back after all that time sitting up. I swear I can feel my spine lengthening . . . in a good way." She breathed out in ecstasy. "Do me a favor?" Laine whispered as the firefighters prepared to walk her to the ambulance.

"Anything," Wes told her immediately.

"See if you can get that damn dog to come to you. I've talked to her for two days straight now. I've become a tad bit attached. Besides, she's hungry and needs a home."

Wes smiled and vaguely heard some of the others chuckling above him. "I'd already planned to. I sort of promised her a big juicy steak."

"You too?"

Wes chuckled, not surprised they were on the same wavelength. "And you might be interested in knowing that the dog is a mommy four times over."

"Really?" Laine's eyes had closed as she was being carried across the field, but they opened to look up at him. Wes was quick to shield them from the harsh sunlight beating down on them. "I saw her when I got out here and figured she was hiding them somewhere. She was scared of me and took off across the field. Stupidly, I wasn't paying attention and stepped right on the boards. As soon as I did, I knew I'd screwed up. I thought she'd take the chance to get the hell away from me. But you know what? She stayed with me the whole time, other than a bit at night when she must've taken a break to feed her puppies. She let me babble to her. I think she kept me sane."

"I wouldn't have even thought to look out here if

it wasn't for her sitting next to your hole," Wes told Laine, still holding her hand as the firefighters continued with their precious bundle across the field. "It looks like we have ourselves a dog."

"*If* you can catch her," Laine said with a hint of the snark he knew and loved.

"If I can catch her," Wes agreed.

They were silent for the rest of the trip to the ambulance and as Moose and Sledge got her settled in the back.

Gesturing to the dog with his head, Wes silently asked Dax to take care of somehow getting the dog to come with him. He'd heard their conversation and nodded, telling Wes he'd get it done.

Watching in disbelief—as all it took was for the other Ranger to open the back door of his car, and the dog jumped right in, joining her puppies now sleeping together on the floor in the backseat—Wes smiled, happy it'd been so easy. Laine would've been devastated if they couldn't help her. Hell, *he* would've been upset about it. He owed the stray everything.

Knowing Dax would have two of the others take care of both his and Laine's vehicles, Wes settled on the bench next to Laine in the ambulance, keeping one hand on her forehead to make sure she didn't feel alone, not even for a moment.

When Sledge got the IV drip going and they were finally bumping their way back down the driveway, Wes blurted out, "I love you."

Laine couldn't turn her head, but her eyes widened as she looked up at him. "What?"

"I love you," he repeated. "When you never showed up at my house and no one knew where you were . . . I knew that my life would never be the same without you in it. We've been hanging out together a lot, and I just assumed we'd continue to do so. Eventually I would've told you how I felt and hopefully we would've gotten married and spent the rest of our lives together. At least that's what I assumed was what would happen.

"But instead, you scared the shit out of me and I never want to feel that way again, ever. I realized that I wouldn't be that frightened if I didn't care about you as much as I did. I love you, Laine. I don't want to wait. I'm one hundred percent sure that you're it for me. It took me forty-two years to find my other half, and now that I have, I'm not letting you go."

"I want to name her Chance."

"What?" Laine's comment was so far away from how he thought she'd respond to his declaration of love and sort-of marriage proposal, he had a hard time switching gears to follow her line of thinking.

"The dog. I want to name her Chance, because without her, we wouldn't have a chance to get married and live happily ever after."

"Okay, darlin'. Chance it is." Wes couldn't help the goofy smile that crept over his face.

"I love you too."

Wes sighed slightly in relief. He didn't think he'd care if she said it back or not, but he did. He cared a lot. He didn't know if she realized that *she* basically asked *him* to marry her, but he was going to hold her to it, no matter what she said later.

"When I was sitting at the bottom of that hole, all I could think of was that I'd never told you and I'd never get a *chance* to tell you. But then I looked up at our stars and knew you were out there somewhere .. . looking for me. And I had no doubt you'd track me down. Although . . . I was kinda hoping it wouldn't have taken so long."

Wes chuckled. "Sorry about that, darlin', it took an expert hacker to figure out the clues you left behind."

"How *did* you find me?"

"I went to your office and saw the names 'Johnson' and 'Morningside' scribbled on your calendar."

"And?"

"And what?"

"That's it?" Laine asked incredulously. "I knew you were good, but I didn't know you were that good."

Wes leaned over and kissed her forehead gently. "When you're feeling better, I'll tell you the whole story. But suffice it to say, you have a lot of friends who busted their asses to do everything they could to find you."

"Thank you." Her words were slurred as the painkillers Sledge pushed through her IV began to take effect.

"Close your eyes and rest now, Laine. I've got you. You're going to be fine."

Laine didn't say another word as she slipped into dreamland, but Wes wasn't expecting it. She was safe, and in relatively good shape for spending two days at the bottom of a well. He wouldn't complain.

13

LAINE SAT on the middle cushion of Wes's large couch surrounded by her friends. Mackenzie and Dax, Cruz and his girlfriend Mickie, Quint and Corrie, Conor, TJ, Hayden, Calder, and even Penelope and Cade from Station 7 were there. When Laine had found out that Sledge's name was Cade, she'd refused to call him by his horrible nickname, proclaiming it 'too silly for such a good looking man.'" Maybe because she wasn't quite up to par after her ordeal, he didn't complain.

Wes had backed away, giving her friends time to see for themselves that she was all right, but Laine knew it was only because he'd had her to himself for the last day. She'd spent twenty-four hours in the hospital for dehydration and for tests, but they'd let her go early the morning before. Her ankles hadn't been broken, only badly sprained, and she'd bounced back quickly after having two bags of IV fluids pushed through her body. Wes hadn't even asked, but had brought her straight to his house and got her settled in his bed, where he'd proceeded to pamper her.

Mack had been waiting at the hospital when they'd brought Laine in. Wes had heard an earful from her about how Dax hadn't let her come with him out to the property. He'd been scared about what they might find and had wanted to spare Mack the possible sight of her best friend dead. But he'd called as soon as Laine had been on the way to the hospital, so she could meet her there.

And she *had* been there. She'd browbeat and badgered the hospital staff enough that they'd let her say a quick few words when Laine had been wheeled in. Enough to satisfy Mack that her friend was indeed all right, and would be fine after everything that had happened.

After arriving back at his place, Wes had cooked a delicious lunch and dinner and brought both to her bedside. They'd watched a couple movies, but her favorite part of being with him was their conversations. She'd told him how she'd felt so alone at the bottom of the well, but that she'd never given up hope that he'd find her. Wes, in turn, admitted that in all his years of being a Texas Ranger, he'd never been so scared he'd screw up a case as much as he was while she'd been missing.

"It gave me a whole new perspective on what the families go through. I remember some of the things I've said to them and it makes me cringe."

"You didn't know." Laine had tried to soothe him.

"I didn't, but that doesn't mean I had the right to be condescending or rude, even if I didn't *know* I was being condescending."

The entire ordeal had brought them closer together, and while she wished it hadn't happened, Laine was pleased with the ultimate outcome.

"I can't believe how different Chance looks, now that you got her cleaned up," Mickie said, commenting on the dog who Wes had brought home while Laine had been in the hospital. She'd been to the groomer and had a thorough bath, her nails clipped, and her ears cleaned. A trip to the vet for a once-over and some shots, and the exhausted but obviously happy dog was currently sleeping in the corner of their bedroom with her puppies, away from the commotion of all the people.

"I know, right? I thought she was a mix when I first saw her, but I can see now she's probably mostly pit bull," Laine said, her voice still a bit lower than usual.

"Are you afraid to have her around?" It was Cade who asked.

"No," Laine said immediately. "I don't care what breed she is. That dog literally saved my life. She didn't show one ounce of aggression at the groomer or the vet, or even when we've been handling her puppies. I think she somehow knows that not only did we save her and her babies, but she saved me too."

Wes told the story only some of the people in his living room had heard. "We were searching the property and I'd begun to think Laine had been snatched away and we'd have to start the search from scratch, when I looked into the pasture and saw Chance sitting there. She wasn't moving, just sitting stock-still. It was unusual and it made me want to know why. If that dog hadn't been out there by that old well, we would've left and never known Laine was there."

Mackenzie put her arm around Laine and hugged her to her side. "I love you, Laine. Don't do that again."

Everyone laughed at the complete seriousness in Mack's voice.

"I won't. From now on, everyone is going to get a complete run-down of my plans for the day . . . every day. Getting up. Drinking coffee. About to shower. Driving to work. Going to X address for a showing. Driving home. Eating dinner."

All the women laughed, the men did not.

"I was kidding," Laine said with a smile, looking at the alpha men staring at her.

"Someday I'll tell you a story about people knowing where you are at all times," Penelope said, fingering the Maltese cross around her neck with a faraway look in her eyes.

"Actually, that's a good idea," Quint agreed with Laine, and she could see him squeeze Corrie's hand. Corrie had her own drama she'd been through . . . kidnapped by loan sharks, and she'd managed to save herself while waiting for Quint to find her. Of *course* he'd agree that it was a good idea to have her text with her whereabouts all day, every day.

"Yeah . . . no," Laine shot back. "Look, it was a freak thing. Just like Mack being buried in that coffin. Or Mickie being in the middle of a turf war between a motorcycle club and a drug lord. The same with Corrie and Penelope being kidnapped. It's not going to happen again."

"Did you hear what you just said?" Conor questioned. "Those things usually don't happen to most people, but the fact that they've happened to four of the most wonderful women—five, if I include you— I've met, who just happened to be dating some of my best friends? Yeah, I think all of you women should make a note of what your plans are every day . . . just in case."

Laine smiled, but hid it behind her hand when she yawned. She probably wouldn't make a list of every second of her day, but she *would* be a bit more careful in the future. She could've saved herself, and Wes, a lot of heartache if she'd only written down the address of the property she was going to, or at least told Rose or Mack where she was going. It had been careless and even a bit reckless on her part, and it wouldn't happen again.

"Laine's tired," Wes said in a firm voice over the din in the room as the women—except for Hayden, who was sitting with her arms crossed as if daring one of her colleagues to suggest she needed to broadcast where she was every second of the day— argued against giving a blow-by-blow of every minute of their plans for the day to their men.

Wes's words were the impetus to get everyone moving. One by one they said their goodbyes to Laine, every single person making sure she knew how happy they were that she was going to be okay.

Penelope gave Laine an extra-long hug when it was her turn. "I'm very glad you're okay. If you ever need to talk to anyone, please let me know. I'm in a group . . . it's for people who've been held hostage, and I know it's different from what happened to you, but it might help if you need it. It's nice to know there are others who are feeling a lot of the same things as you."

"You okay?" Laine asked. She wasn't that close to Penelope, but she'd met her a few times and really liked her. She was a firecracker and tough as a whip, but she somehow put out vulnerable vibes at the same time.

"Yeah. I'm okay. Some days are better than others. I was serious about the group. There are people who have gone through a lot of shit, and they're amazing. One of my best friends in the group has to attend electronically now, but she's working on her issues. It makes what you and I went through look like a walk in the park."

Laine's interest was piqued. "Worse than what you went through?"

"Yeah. She moved here from California. She'd been kidnapped by a serial killer. A SEAL team rescued her and another woman before the sicko could kill them, but he'd had her long enough to make her life a living hell. She has problems leaving her house now as a result. It all sucks. She was doing really well, but recently she's been having issues getting to the meetings in person, so I set it up so she could attend remotely."

Laine wanted to ask more, to get to know more about what the poor woman had gone through and how she was doing, but another yawn broke through before she could comment.

Penelope gave her another long hug then pulled back again. "Okay, I'll let you go. I'm glad you're all right, Laine."

"Thanks, Penelope. See you later?"

"Definitely."

Wes put his arm around Laine as they waved to everyone from the doorway. Finally, when they were all gone, he pulled them inside and closed and locked the door.

Feeling more tired than she thought she'd be, Laine didn't protest as Wes helped her walk into his bedroom. He got her settled and said, "Let me take Chance out, now that the coast is clear. I'll be back."

"Okay." Laine held out her hand and Chance came over to the side of the bed and licked at it, before she and her four puppies followed Wes out of the room.

Laine snuggled down into the covers and closed her eyes.

She felt when Wes returned and climbed in behind her. He was warm against her back and the arm around her waist held her tightly to him.

"I love you," Wes murmured as he kissed her ear.

Laine turned to her back and smiled up at the handsome man above her. "I love you too."

"Will you marry me?"

Laine wasn't all that surprised at the question. She'd basically already told him she wanted to spend the rest of her life with him while they were out at the Johnson property, after Squirrel had hauled her out of the hole, but it felt good to make it official. "Yes."

"Good. When?"

"Whenever you want."

"Really?"

"Really."

"Tomorrow?"

"Uh . . . excuse me?"

"Tomorrow. We can go to the courthouse and do it."

"Don't we have to get a license and sit out the waiting period and all of that?" Laine asked.

"Damn. Yeah, I think it's seventy-two hours or something."

"What's the hurry? I'm not going anywhere," Laine soothed, running her hand up and down his biceps.

"When I realized how much I love you and how precious life is, I recognized that our time here on earth is just too short. I want to spend every second of the time I have left with you."

"We can do that and not be married," Laine said reasonably. She wasn't trying to talk Wes out of it, but was trying to understand the urgency he was feeling.

"I want my ring on your finger, and I'm hoping you'll change your name to King. But I would totally understand if you didn't want to. It's kind of archaic that the woman has to be the one to change her name, but I can't help that it would make me feel good."

"Laine King. It sounds good," she mused.

"It sounds fucking fantastic," Wes agreed, then leaned down to kiss her.

"As soon as the three days go by, I'll marry you. Although . . . Mack is gonna lose her mind if she's not invited. And probably Mickie and Corrie too. And I wouldn't want to do it without your friends there. Oh, and Squirrel and Moose and Penelope, and all the others from the fire station too. We can't leave them out."

Wes laughed. "How about we have a nice quiet civil ceremony then have a big-ass party later?"

"Deal. I want to make love to you, Wes." When he opened his mouth to speak, Laine put her finger on his lips to shush him and continued, "But I'm still too sore. Just the *thought* of spreading my legs is enough to make me wanna hurl, imagining the pressure it'd put on my hips. But as soon as I'm feeling up to it, you had better watch out. I'm gonna jump you."

Wes chuckled. "I'll look forward to it, darlin'. I'm perfectly content to hold you close all night and every night until you're healed enough."

"Maybe in the barn . . . can we reenact that moment when we first saw each other? I'd love to act out my vivid dreams of running across the barn and taking you to the ground and having my way with you," Laine told Wes with a smirk. "That rope and your cowboy hat have played front and center in a lot of my fantasies as well. I swear to God, the first thing I thought when I saw you standing there without your shirt on and your V-muscles leading to my Promised Land, was that you were the most amazing specimen of a man I'd ever seen in my life."

"You too?" Wes asked with a grin. "That was *my* fantasy. Not my abs, but pulling you into my arms, stripping off your top so I could get a good look at those tits and the nipples that stood up to say hello to me, and taking you right there against the wall in my barn."

"I'm so glad I didn't back out of coming to watch that photography session that day. It changed my life . . . for the better."

"Mine too." Wes kissed Laine, making sure she kept still so as not to hurt herself. "I got the photos from that day back from Jack. I'm supposed to pick my favorite three. I forgot about it until now. Will you help me choose?"

"Oh, shit yeah. I want you to be the hottest man in that calendar, but I was serious when I told you back then that I'd prefer for you to be all mine. I'll let others drool over your body, but your face is all mine. My very own Texas Ranger cowboy. I love you, more than you'll ever know."

"I know, because I love you like that too. Sleep

now. Tomorrow is the first day of the rest of our lives."

Look for the next book in the Badge of Honor Series: *Shelter for Elizabeth*. You first met Beth in *Protecting Summer*...she has since moved to Texas to try to deal with being kidnapped by Ben Hurst...and meets a sexy firefighter who just might help her with her phobias.

If you want to know more about Penelope, the Army Princess, and her ordeal of being kidnapped by ISIS, please check out *Protecting the Future*.

JOIN my Newsletter and find out about sales, free books, contests and new releases before anyone else!! Click HERE

Want to know when my books go on sale? Follow me on Bookbub HERE!

Would you like Susan's Book Protecting Caroline for FREE?
Click HERE

Also by Susan Stoker

Badge of Honor: Texas Heroes Series

Justice for Mackenzie

Justice for Mickie

Justice for Corrie

Justice for Laine (novella)

Shelter for Elizabeth

Justice for Boone

Shelter for Adeline

Shelter for Sophie

Justice for Erin

Justice for Milena

Shelter for Blythe

Justice for Hope

Shelter for Quinn

Shelter for Koren

Shelter for Penelope

Delta Team Two Series

Shielding Gillian

Shielding Kinley (Aug 2020)

Shielding Aspen (Oct 2020)

Shielding Riley (Jan 2021)

Shielding Devyn (May 2021)

Shielding Ember (Sept 2021)
Shielding Sierra (TBA)

Delta Force Heroes Series

Rescuing Rayne
Rescuing Aimee (novella)
Rescuing Emily
Rescuing Harley
Marrying Emily (novella)
Rescuing Kassie
Rescuing Bryn
Rescuing Casey
Rescuing Sadie (novella)
Rescuing Wendy
Rescuing Mary
Rescuing Macie (novella)

SEAL of Protection: Legacy Series

Securing Caite
Securing Brenae (novella)
Securing Sidney
Securing Piper
Securing Zoey
Securing Avery (May 2020)
Securing Kalee (Sept 2020)
Securing Jane (novella) (Feb 2021)

SEAL Team Hawaii Series

Finding Elodie (Apr 2021)

Finding Lexie (Aug 2021)

Finding Kenna (Oct 2021)

Finding Monica (TBA)

Finding Carly (TBA)

Finding Ashlyn (TBA)

Ace Security Series

Claiming Grace

Claiming Alexis

Claiming Bailey

Claiming Felicity

Claiming Sarah

Mountain Mercenaries Series

Defending Allye

Defending Chloe

Defending Morgan

Defending Harlow

Defending Everly

Defending Zara

Defending Raven (June 2020)

Silverstone Series

Trusting Skylar (Dec 2020)

Trusting Taylor (Mar 2021)
Trusting Molly (July 2021)
Trusting Cassidy (Dec 2021

SEAL of Protection Series
Protecting Caroline
Protecting Alabama
Protecting Fiona
Marrying Caroline (novella)
Protecting Summer
Protecting Cheyenne
Protecting Jessyka
Protecting Julie (novella)
Protecting Melody
Protecting the Future
Protecting Kiera (novella)
Protecting Alabama's Kids (novella)
Protecting Dakota

Stand Alone
The Guardian Mist
Nature's Rift
A Princess for Cale
A Moment in Time- A Collection of Short Stories
Lambert's Lady

Special Operations Fan Fiction

http://www.AcesPress.com

Beyond Reality Series

Outback Hearts

Flaming Hearts

Frozen Hearts

Writing as Annie George:

Stepbrother Virgin (erotic novella)

ABOUT THE AUTHOR

New York Times, *USA Today* and *Wall Street Journal* Bestselling Author Susan Stoker has a heart as big as the state of Texas where she lives, but this all American girl has also spent the last fourteen years living in Missouri, California, Colorado, and Indiana. She's married to a retired Army man who now gets to follow *her* around the country.

She debuted her first series in 2014 and quickly followed that up with the SEAL of Protection Series, which solidified her love of writing and creating stories readers can get lost in.

If you enjoyed this book, or any book, please consider leaving a review. It's appreciated by authors more than you'll know.

www.stokeraces.com

susan@stokeraces.com